ANTHONY D. FARR

Published by arrangement with the author.

Copyright © 2024 by Anthony D. Farr.

All rights reserved.

To Dan:
Thank you for always being my biggest fan and my favorite reader.
I miss you.

Contents

Introduction

Thanks so much for taking the time to read my stories. These stories take place in the fictional town of Raven's Bend, Maine. For those who don't know, Raven's Bend is based on the Lewiston/Auburn area of Maine, so if you're familiar with those places, you might find something in this collection that tickles your memory.

Also, below is a QR code that will take you to a curated playlist to enhance the reading experience. I hope you enjoy.

I hope you find something you like. If you do, be sure to let me know.

Thanks,
Anthony

The Woman at the Mill

The storm last night had been cold. Cold and wild with the kind of wind that finds its way through every crack and crevice of both old and new buildings, indiscriminate of every effort to prevent the cold from taking hold inside. That cold rested over the quaint river town of Raven's Bend, Maine. The Bend, as locals called it, lay nestled beneath a blanket of heavy wet snow, glowing a blinding white in the morning sun.

Mason Reid covered his eyes as he ducked out of the homeless shelter, hoisting his green, oversized duffle bag higher on his shoulder. Patrick Dupree, the unlucky worker whose duty it was to get everyone out, clapped him on the shoulder and gave him a knowing nod, as if to say, "I'm sorry you can't stay." Mason gave a curt nod in return and stepped out into the brisk, bright morning air. He could come back at dusk, which these days happened close to four in the afternoon, but for now, he had to find somewhere to duck away from the sharp biting wind.

The last vestiges of the Nor'easter blew through the old mill town, dragging the cold air from the canal over the street and straight through Mason's old, tattered jacket. He zipped it, covering his exposed face, and pushed into the wind as he made his way down the hard-packed sidewalk, already cleared by the intrepid city workers who braved the early morning sub-freezing temperatures to ready Raven's Bend for the day.

The town was still asleep as he made his way down the hill toward the center of town and the river beyond. A few early risers were out walking their dogs or shoveling sidewalks, but most people remained bundled up in their homes, sipping coffee and enjoying a slow start to the day. The snow crunched beneath his boots, each step taking him closer to Main Street and the businesses that lined either side.

City Hall's tower loomed ahead and to the left, its face illuminated by spotlights, even in this early sunlight. It was one of Mason's favorite places in town. He loved to sit on one of the benches ringing the nearby park and watch the world go by. But today, really, since the deep winter had set in, Mason had other plans.

Get warm. Stay warm.

Those were his priorities for the day. He still had half a turkey sub a random stranger had given him yesterday. Mason was hoping to make it last for at least a few days.

The wind picked up as he crossed the street, sending a chill through him that made him shiver involuntarily. His breath came out in frosty puffs that quickly dissipated in the air. He shoved his hands into his pockets and hunched his shoulders, trying to make himself as small as possible. He stared across the street at the brick archway leading down to one of his favorite places in this town.

The black and white sign above the arch read, *"Blind Date Books."*

The bookshop was one of his favorite places to go when he had extra cash on hand. It was always warm and smelled like coffee and old books. He could spend hours in there, looking at the different titles and flipping through the pages of whatever caught his eye. Before crossing the street, he spied a sandwich board in the archway that dropped his heart.

Closed. Snow Day!

Turning back to the sidewalk, Mason continued down the main drag of the town.

The cold air numbed his face and hands, despite his efforts to keep them tucked away. He knew he needed to find some place warm soon or he wouldn't make it through the day. His stomach growled, reminding him of the half a sandwich he had stashed away in his duffle. He considered eating it now but decided against it. He may need it later.

He walked past *Donovan's Marvelous Masks*, a small shop that always had its door open and tinkling bells announcing customers. It was one of those places that was always busy, no matter what time of day it was. People were always coming and going, browsing the racks of colorful masks or chatting with the owner, Paul Delacrux. Mason missed Donovan, the previous owner who died just last Halloween. He always had a job for Mason and never turned down his company. He wondered now if Paul had the same philosophy but decided not to test his luck and pushed deeper into the town toward the falls.

The river was always louder this time of year, the water rushing over the rocks as it made its way under the ice, encrusting the falls. The sound was soothing, despite the frigid temperatures. As he got closer, he could see the snow-covered rooftops of the buildings next to the falls. They were mostly abandoned now, but in their heyday, they were part of a thriving mill town. He could imagine what it must have been like back then, with the mill operating day and night and the town busting at the seams with people.

Now, most of the mills lay vacant except for businesses making use of the space for back-office workers and a few niche restaurants. Some said these buildings were haunted, but Mason was not one to believe in ghosts.

He rounded the corner, and the falls came into view. The snow-covered rocks and icicles hanging from the edge of the waterfall sparkled in the sunlight. It was a beautiful sight, but one that did little to ease the chill he felt. He needed to find some place to go and soon.

The old mill loomed ahead and to the right, its windows boarded up and doors sealed shut. It had been abandoned for over half a century. But Mason knew there was a way in. He had found it by accident one day when he was exploring in the Fall. The main entrance stood locked and barred, but he had found a loose board near the back that led him into a small room that must have once been an office of some sort.

Finding the loose board, he pulled it to the side, giving him just enough room to enter. He squeezed through the opening, making himself as small as possible. The mill was dark and musty, but still somehow familiar to him. He had walked through the halls countless times in his mind, imagining what it must have been like for someone who actually worked here day after day.

The main room, once full of workers and the sounds of heavy machinery, was now empty. He could almost hear the rumble of the machines, almost feel the vibrations under his feet. His heart pounded in his chest as he continued, exploring every nook and cranny until he found himself standing in front of a set of stairs leading up to an upper level.

Mason hesitated for only a moment before beginning his ascent. He had to see it, had to know what was at the top. The stairwell seemed to go on forever but finally ended at a door with a small window near the top that let in just enough light from outside that he could make out a large open space beyond it.

He took a deep breath, then slowly lifted his hand and grasped the knob, turning it ever so gently until he felt it give way beneath his touch. Holding his breath, Mason pushed open the door and stepped out onto the top floor of the mill. The view was breath-taking, overlooking all of town and even stretching to the river before disappearing into thick forest beyond. Sighing contentedly, Mason sank down onto a broken desk in front of the window, taking in everything he saw before him.

Up here, the windows remained unbroken, and very little of the wind made its way into the old office. Mason grew comfortable, almost forgetting that he was still in the middle of a deep freeze. As he gazed out over the town, he could feel time slowing around him, as if nothing else was real but this moment, this place. Here in the mill, everything seemed forgotten and at peace. It was just what Mason needed to relax finally and escape from the cold for a little while.

That and a fire.

He stood, dusting off his pants before walking to the small wood stove in the corner. It looked ancient, like a long-forgotten relic of days gone by, but there was still a decent amount of wood piled up next to it. He set about lighting a fire, using some old newspapers he found, and soon had a nice blaze going. The fire crackled and popped, wafting heat over Mason's face as he watched the flames dance and twine around each other, throwing shadows on the dusty walls of the mill.

Sitting back down in front of the window, Mason warmed his hands and feet and watched as the sun rose higher, painting the sky in a crystal-clear blue only found in the sky of a Maine winter. He closed his eyes and slowly inhaled, letting the warmth seep into his bones. He didn't want to leave this place, didn't want to leave this moment. But he knew it wouldn't last forever.

So instead, he would linger for as long as he could, enjoying every minute of his fleeting respite from the harsh winter world outside of the mill.

The sound of the door opening below startled him and he leapt to his feet, heart racing as he tried to think of a way to explain his presence if someone caught him. But as he heard footsteps coming up the stairs, he realized there was nowhere to hide. He would have to face whoever it was head on.

Mason steeled himself, heart still pounding in his chest as the footsteps grew closer and closer until they finally stopped just outside the door. He held his breath, not sure what to expect as the door slowly opened and an attractive young woman stepped into the room. She stood taller than Mason, slender, with dark shoulder-length hair and deep green eyes. Her narrow face, firm jaw, and high cheekbones cast stark shadows from the firelight. She wore a long red coat reaching down to her ankles. Her scruffy black boots softly sifted the dust as she entered the room.

She looked around, her gaze darting around the room before landing on Mason.

"Hello," she said, voice flowing and gentle like soft music. "I'm sorry if I startled you. I did not know I had company today."

Mason let out a breath he didn't know he was holding and shook his head. "It's okay," he said. "I didn't know there was anyone here. If you've claimed this place, I can find somewhere else."

The woman laughed softly. "Of course not," she said, walking towards him and settling down on the desk next to him. She looked out at the view, a soft smile playing on her lips as she gazed out over the town. "I'm Cora," she said, holding out her hand for Mason to shake.

Mason nodded and took her hand in his, shaking it firmly. "I'm Mason."

Cora smiled again and turned back towards the window, watching as the sun continued to rise higher in the sky.

"It's beautiful here," she murmured, almost to herself. "So peaceful."

Mason nodded in agreement and watched as Cora leaned forward slightly, taking everything in before sighing contentedly and sinking into the ancient wooden chair. He felt drawn to this enigmatic woman. A strange warmth spreading through him as he watched her watching him with dark eyes full of life and mystery.

"I'm just staying the day. I won't get in your way. I promise. Once the shelter opens back up, I'm back in there for the night," Mason said, leaning against the wall. "Do you have somewhere warm to stay tonight?"

"I have to stay here," Cora whispered, brushing her hand through the thick dust on the armrests of her chair. "This is a thin place, and if I'm not careful, the stories will bleed through."

Mason frowned, not quite understanding. "Stories?" he asked.

"Yes," Cora said, looking back out at the view. "Stories. Tales. They get trapped here sometimes, in places like this."

Mason felt a chill run down his spine, and he shifted uncomfortably. "Places like what?" He asked.

Cora laughed softly, the sound like tinkling glass. "This place," she paused, drumming her fingers on the desk, then continued, "Places like this town have scars, deep scars. They carry a weight through generations. It's a deep magic that runs through places like this." She turned back to Mason then, her eyes piercing in the firelight. "Do you believe in ghosts, Mason?" she asked softly.

Mason swallowed hard and shook his head. "No," he said firmly. "I don't."

Cora nodded slowly; her expression thoughtful. "I used to not believe in them. At least not until I came here. Then I learned the truth."

"What truth?" Mason asked. He knew he should not engage, but he felt at ease with Cora.

"Ghosts don't exist. At least not how I used to think of them. Echoes remain. Echoes of the past, present, and future. Echoes of possibilities. That's what our stories are. We are giving voice to the echoes of the hidden stories of the universe."

Mason frowned, still not quite understanding. Cora sighed and leaned back in her chair, steepling her fingers in front of her.

"It's like this," she said. "There is a place beyond this world that we can't see. It's a place of infinite potential and possibility. All the stories that have ever been or will be exist there. In that place, they are just echoes waiting to be given voice."

"And that's what you do? You give voice to the echoes?" Mason asked.

Cora nodded. "Yes," she whispered. "I give voice to the echoes." She breathed deep of the chilly air. "That's why I like this town. So many stories to tell. This place is a thin place. The stories come easier here. It's easier to find them. And once they are told, it keeps them from bleeding through."

"Bleeding through? What do you mean?"

"The place our stories come from has been sick for a long time. In the thin places, if the stories aren't given voice, then they can become real, especially on nights like last night. The storm gave the echoes more power. They aren't malicious or evil but can give life to malicious entities and cause harm to the real world."

"That's absurd," Mason chuckled, "is that true of all stories?" He raised an eyebrow at Cora as he waited for her answer. "And what happened last night? I think I would have heard if something went down in town last night."

Cora laughed; a hint of a crystal wind chime tinkled beneath her voice.

"Mason, last night, many stories came through, but most folks ignore them. Preferring to believe something more in line with how they choose to perceive reality. Maybe by telling them to you now, I can take any remaining power away from them. Would you be willing to listen for a bit? Humor an old woman?"

"Sure," Mason nodded. It was not like he had anywhere better to be.

"Tend your fire, and I'll tell you all that transpired last night, and when I'm finished, you can tell me if you believe me."

Mason stoked the fire, his curiosity piqued by Cora's words. He settled back in his chair, preparing to listen to her tale.

Cora spoke, her voice soft and melodic, "As I said, this town is built on scars. Scars of violence and trauma running deep through the psyche of Raven's Bend. There are stories that react to that kind of trauma, and last night, they came bubbling to the surface. I could hear them in the wind, see them in the shadows. Screaming faces caught in mid-air, tumbling end over end down an invisible staircase. A woman wailing for her husband, her mouth open in a silent gasp of grief. A pale man, hungry and staring into the whiteout of the blizzard." Cora paused, her eyes distant, remembering what she saw last night. "It was horrible, but also beautiful," she whispers finally. "And now, by sharing with you, maybe some peace will come to these stories."

"So, tell me then, what happened last night?" Mason said with a skeptical tone to his voice.

Cora nodded and continued, her voice growing stronger as she fell into a trance-like state.

As she spoke, Mason found himself drawn in by the words, caught up in the ebb and flow of Cora's storytelling. Images formed and danced in his vision, and he felt the tempestuous energy of the storm thrumming around him as she gave voice to the tales from the previous night.

"It began, like all things do on nights like last night. It all began before the storm. Early in the afternoon at the Big Apple on Main Street, in fact. As Daisy Morrow pumped gas into her car, she gazed into the distance. On the horizon stood dark omens of the coming Nor'Easter..."

In the Loop

As Daisy Marrow pumped gas into her white '94 Honda Civic, she gazed into the distance. On the horizon stood dark omens of the coming Nor'Easter. Daisy's thick glasses magnified the brown of her eyes like those of a deer on alert at the forest's edge. Her hair, once a fiery red, was now beige from lack of dye for several months. Her skin, tan and healthy during the summer, was now pale, her freckles more a memory than a characteristic, and tended to disappear in the dead of a Maine winter. She pulled her flannel L.L. Bean jacket tighter as the cold crept over her before the coming storm.

The town of Raven's Bend was a small, close-knit community split down the middle by the Androscoggin River. The Bend, as locals called it, was in the midst of a cold snap, and the smell of wood-burning fireplaces and wood smoke hung in the air. The only sound echoing through the town was the wind whipping down Main Street. Raven's Bend's small community was usually bustling, but the cold dampened all the activity. As she walked from her car to the gas station, her footsteps crunched in the early snow in advance of the coming blizzard. The chill ate through her jeans and flannel, and she smiled at the blast of heat as she entered the gas station.

Doug, a ruddy-haired teen with a severe case of acne ravaging his pock-marked face, smiled, showing off his new braces courtesy of the one and only dentist in town.

"Afternoon, Daisy," he smiled bigger as she entered. Just eight years ago, Daisy had been his babysitter to make some extra cash before she graduated, and Doug had a childhood crush on her. She thought he was over it, but some remnants of his professed undying love seemed to remain.

"Afternoon, Doug," she returned his smile as she perused the coolers for a Dr. Pepper.

"So, the Nor'Easter's gonna be a doozy, huh?" he asked as she placed her soda onto the counter and a few drops of condensation splattered on the plastic top.

"It looks like it," Daisy nodded. "Be sure to get out of here and get home before the worst of it runs through town."

Doug grinned widely. "You know it. I ain't staying here longer than necessary. As soon as my shift is done, I'm gone." He rang her items and swiveled the small display on the register. It blazed red digital numbers reading $21.22. "What are you up to tonight? Going to batten down the hatches in your apartment?"

"Something like that," she said, sliding a twenty and a five over to him. She did not have the heart to tell him the truth. That this might be the last time he ever saw her. If she had her way, this would be her last stop in Raven's Bend.

"You going to be okay tonight?" Doug smiled his broad grin again, but a well of pity pooled in his eyes.

"Yeah. Yeah, I'll be fine," she nodded her head and took her change. Doug meant well. They all did, but she could not deal with that look.

"Have a good one," Doug called after her, and she waved back, knowing he would stare at the door long after she left.

Outside, the biting wind whipped around her like an angry ghost. The early flakes of snow stung and bit into her skin and her face as she made her way back to her car. But she was not alone. The wind hissed and moaned, a warning of the shit to come. It whispered into her ear a warning of the Nor'Easter.

As she drove through town, she could not help but notice how quiet it was. The usual early morning voices and sounds were missing, replaced by the clamoring of bits of ice on the road. Only the very stupid or very desperate were out before this storm. Daisy was unsure which of the two she was. All she knew was she had to leave this town. And it had to be today.

The first flakes fell heavier now, and the windshield wipers worked at full speed, but it was not enough. She could barely see ten feet in front of her. The early snow coming down so fast and furious slicked the roads before the plows had a chance to make a dent in it. Deserted roads greeted her as she made her way out of town, and soon she was on the ramp, taking her away. Away. The word echoed in her head like a broken record. Raven's Bend was not her home. Not since Oliver died. She grew up here, but this town was not home until she met Oliver. He made this home, but without him, the Bend was too much.

She crept along the road, going slower than she ever had before, not wanting to take any chances with this weather. She knew all too well how quickly conditions could deteriorate out here. And she did not want to end up buried in the ditch.

The windshield wipers swooshed back and forth, and Daisy's heartbeat in time with them. Back and forth. Back and forth. It was a mantra to keep her focused on the road. She did not want to think about what this journey meant. She just wanted to get out in one piece.

The snow continued to fall, and the roads grew slicker by the minute, but Daisy soldiered on. She had to reach her destination before the storm got too bad.

Finally, after what felt like hours, but in reality, was only a few minutes, she reached the on-ramp for I 95, headed south. The interstate would take her far away from this place. Her heart ached as she drove away from all she had ever known, but she knew it was for the best. She could not stay here any longer. It was time to start fresh somewhere new. As she drove, the blizzard picked up. Visibility dropped to nothing as snow swirled in every direction, coating her windshield and hiding everything outside of her car. She drove, watching intently the mile markers popping up briefly to her right as momentary breaks in the white wall of the snow.

As the storm raged on, the mile markers repeated. They blurred together as Daisy struggled to see where she was going. She was lost out here in this vast white expanse, and there seemed no way out. But she pressed on. She could not stop now.

The howling of the wind grew louder as snow continued to pile up around her car, weighing it down like an angry ghost. The cold bit deep into her skin and froze her to the bone, but despite it all, she kept pushing forward. For Oliver. For herself. She was done with Raven's Bend forever, and no Maine blizzard would keep her from leaving this town finally behind her once and for all.

After an hour of driving, Daisy felt an unease creep into the pit of her stomach. Mile marker fourteen blinked in and out in the white wall of flying snow. Daisy slowed to less than a crawl. She realized this was the third time she had passed the same mile marker.

A feeling of dread overtook her, and she pulled to the side of the road, coming to a stop. She could not go any further. It was as if the turnpike had become a giant circle, and she was caught in its middle, going around and around with no way out.

Desperate, Daisy got out of her car, wading through the snow that was now above her ankles. She trudged a few steps away from her car, scanning for any headlights or the sound of a plow. Nothing rose above the roar of the storm or shone through the stinging white of the snow. Scared and defeated, Daisy made her way back to her car and climbed inside. She pulled back onto the highway, determined to keep going and get as far away from Raven's Bend as she could.

"Must have just gotten turned around on the pike," she whispered to herself.

As she drove on, mile marker fourteen continued to appear and disappear in the driving snow. Again and again. Over and over. She gripped her steering wheel until her knuckles grew white and she bit her lip hard enough to draw blood.

"Wake up. Wake up. Wake up!" She shouted to her empty car. "Wake up," her voice trailed off as her eyes dropped to the dials on the dashboard.

The gas gauge.

It had not moved in the hours she had been driving. She should have used half a tank by now, but the needle still hovered at the full line. She looked outside at the empty highway surrounding her. No cars or plows had passed in either direction since she started driving. She was the only one out here, and yet somehow, she wasn't running out of gas.

Daisy's heart sank. The town was cursed. She could never leave. The Bend wanted to keep her here forever, just like it had kept Oliver.

Tears fell from Daisy's eyes as she pounded her fists on the steering wheel in frustration. She was so close to getting away. So close to finally escaping this place and starting over. But now it seemed as if she would be stuck here forever, just like Oliver.

She pulled over to the side of the road and stopped as the wheels crunched in the deep snow.

"I just miss you so damn much," Daisy whispered as she leaned her head into her hands.

"Hey, Daze," Oliver's voice drifted to her from the passenger seat, "I miss you too."

Daisy looked up slowly, her eyes starting at the floorboard, and saw Oliver's L.L. Bean boots, his deep blue jeans with the bottom tucked into the tops of his boots like he always did. As she lifted her gaze further, she saw his checkered red and black flannel; the sleeves rolled up just below his elbows. Even higher, and she saw the smile that melted her heart. Oliver's boyish smile was set on his smooth face, and it broke even wider as she looked into his kind eyes.

"O?" She choked. "Is... is that really you?"

"In the flesh," Oliver replied with a wink. "Or maybe not. To be honest, I'm not sure."

"But... but how? I mean... you're really here? But I'm not dreaming?" Daisy asked, still not quite convinced this was really happening.

"If you're dreaming, then I am too," Oliver said with a shrug. "But yeah. It's really me."

"How is this possible? The last time I saw you was..." Daisy trailed off as the memories of that awful day came crashing back. The day she lost Oliver in the car accident.

Oliver reached out and took her hand, giving it a squeeze. "I know, Daze. I know it's been tough without me."

"You have no idea," Daisy said, her voice cracking as she fought back tears. "Every day is so hard without you. I don't know how to do this by myself."

"You're doing just fine, babe," Oliver said softly as he brushed away a tear that had slipped down her cheek. "You're one of the strongest people I know."

"I don't feel very strong right now," Daisy admitted with a trembling voice.

"That's because you've been carrying this all on your own for too long," Oliver said gently. "It's time to let others in again."

Daisy nodded as he pulled her into a hug. She wrapped her arms around him and buried her face in her hands as she cried for all she had lost and for everything left unsaid between them.

"Promise me it's you. Promise," she whispered into his flannel.

"The one and only," Oliver said as he unbuckled his seatbelt and pulled her closer.

"But... how?" Daisy asked as she clung to him tightly, afraid he would disappear if she let go.

"I told you I would always find you, no matter what," Oliver said as he brushed the hair out of her face. "I will always be with you, Daze. I promise."

"I'm so sorry, O. I'm so sorry about that day and the things I said to you. I'm so sorry." Daisy's words flew from her mouth in rapid fire, almost merging into an incoherent jumble.

"Sshhh," Oliver hushed her as he rocked her gently. "It's okay, Daze. I understand."

"No, it's not okay," Daisy said as she pulled back to look at him. "You died because of me, and I can never forgive myself for that."

"Hey, now," Oliver said as he cupped her face in his hands. "None of that is your fault, do you hear me? It was an accident and there is nothing you could have done to change it. So please, stop beating yourself up about it."

"I just can't, O. I can't do it. It's so hard." Daisy hung her head.

"I know, babe," Oliver said as he pulled her close again. "But you are one of the strongest people I know, okay? You've got this. I have faith in you."

"Thank you," Daisy whispered as she clung to him, feeling comforted by his words.

"Anytime, Daze," Oliver said, his voice falling faintly in the distance between them. He pulled her tight with a quick squeeze, then pushed her away so he could look into her eyes. "I need you to do one thing for me."

"Anything," she replied, with eyes wide and cheeks wet.

"I need you to go back to the Bend," he whispered.

"I can't," Daisy looked at him in confusion. "Why?"

"You can't leave like this. Not running from something. Not running from me and what happened."

"I'm not running from you," Daisy said quickly. "I'm just… I don't know if I can go back there, O. I don't know if I can face it."

"You can do this, Daze," Oliver said firmly. "I have faith in you, and if you want to leave the Bend and make a life elsewhere, you do that, but do it on your own terms. Not because the grief is too much, and it forces you to run out on a night like tonight." He gestured to the white wall of snow flowing around her car.

"Will you stay with me?" She asked, her voice breaking.

"I will. But not like this. I'll always be with you, Daze. But I need you to be strong for yourself. You, Daze. You've got this."

Tears spilled from her eyes as she leaned back into her seat.

"I've got to go back, don't I?"

Oliver nodded.

"O, I don't know if I can. I can't go back to the Bend," she whimpered.

"I know," he whispered.

"But I can't leave you. I don't want to leave you."

Oliver took her hand and squeezed it reassuringly.

"You have to, Daze," he said firmly. "I will always be with you, no matter what happens. But you need to go back for yourself, for your own sake. You don't have to stay, but don't leave like this. If you need to go, make it on your own terms."

Daisy nodded slowly, still trembling from the weight of her grief.

"Okay," she whispered as she turned the key in the ignition and turned the key. The car protested as the engine sputtered alive, grumbling against the cold. She looked outside her window at the snow piling up against the side of her car. "O, I don't think I'll be able to make it home," she turned her head to find Oliver gone. His seat empty. Not even an impression left from his body. Daisy closed her eyes tight as tears spilled down her cheeks.

The car shook, less from the wind, and more from a vibration coming from beneath Daisy's feet. She looked in the mirror, wiping her eyes, as a wall of dirty yellow headlights burst through the thick white veil of the snow.

Daisy wiped her tears as she stared at the plow behind her car. For a moment, it was just a blur of yellow and white snow in the night. The plow chugged forward, slowly pushing the snow to the side and revealing a clear path for Daisy's car. Before she could pull into the cleared path, the plow lurched to a lumbering halt.

The plow driver jumped down from his cab and walked over to Daisy's window. She recognized Tim Lesae's lime green Adidas sweatshirt as he trudged toward her car through the stinging wind. She cracked her window as he got closer, his brown eyes visible between his thick gray face mask and orange knit cap.

"You okay?" he asked gruffly, but the edges of his mask lifted, showing a smile buried beneath the layers. Steam poured from deep within the fabric.

"Yeah," Daisy replied, swallowing hard to keep herself together. "I'm fine."

He squinted as he came within arm's length of the car.

"Daisy? What the hell are you doing out here on a night like tonight? Turnpike is greasy all the way from here to Kennebunkport. You ain't going anywhere on a night like this."

Daisy laughed, a half sob wrenched from her chest.

"You know me, just going for an evening drive, and now I just need to get back to the Bend."

"Well, then follow me back to the exit."

With a gentle pat on her car and an understanding wink, Tim returned to the plow. He honked the horn twice and flashed his lights. With a forceful push of his plow into the deep snow, he started forward, sending it flying in waves around him as he drove into the storm.

Daisy watched him pull off with a deep sigh of relief. She gunned the gas and pulled in behind Tim's plow as he cleared a path for her. At the next gap in the median, Tim looped around to the northbound lane of the Turnpike and headed back to Raven's Bend. Daisy followed closely, keeping his taillights visible as the storm obscured everything else.

Eventually, Tim pulled off and the green exit sign reading Exit 13 swam into view from the depths of the gray swirl of the snow. Daisy followed him up the exit ramp into Raven's Bend and turned onto Lewiston Road toward downtown.

Toward her apartment.

Toward home.

Tim honked again as he returned to the Turnpike, leaving Daisy to make it home on her own. As Daisy drove, the snow continued to fall, blanketing the city in white and quieting all sound around her. There were no other cars on the road and the snow blanketed everything in soft layers. As she turned onto her street, Daisy felt a sense of peace settle over her, warming her from the inside out as she pulled into her parking spot with a plume of white steam hovering above her car like a protective shield.

Daisy exited her car and made her way through the thick snow to her door. The darkness and cold of her apartment greeted her like a tomb. But it was a peaceful, familiar tomb. And now she knew it was not a weight that had to dictate her life. Stay or go in the Bend; it was her choice. She would not run.

She had made it through so much here in the Bend. Despite her grief and sadness; she had now found her strength once again. And for that, she was grateful to have been stuck by the side of the road alongside Oliver—even if only for a little while. That feeling—Oliver beside her in the car in the midst of the Nor'Easter—would remain with her forever no matter if she stayed in the Bend or not.

Bread and Milk

"Come on, you two, we've gotta get down to the store before everything is gone!" Pricilla Humphrey changed out of her scrubs, tossing her Saint Damian's badge, and pulled on long underwear, jeans, a flannel, and an oversized coat with the flawless and smooth perfection of one who has done this routine many times. Her boys, Conner and Richard, chased each other around the apartment in differing stages of "ready." Connor lurched around with one boot on and his hooded coat trailing off his head as he bounded after his younger brother. Richard, still in his pajamas, but wearing both boots, screamed with laughter as his pursuer gained ground rounding the corner into the kitchen.

"Bull's eye!" Connor crowed as he grabbed his brother in a headlock and gave him a noogie.

"Cut it out!" Richard squealed, trying to break free. Connor continued without mercy on his younger sibling. "Stop. Now," Richard said flatly.

Connor stopped abruptly and released Richard with a confused look on his face. Their mother sighed as she scooped the two of them up in her arms.

"I don't know why I bother." But she smiled as she held them down and finished dressing them. The smile remained as she loaded them into the car, listening to their laughter echoing in the small space.

The drive to the store was made in silence, broken only by the scraping of windshield wipers and an occasional "Wow!" as a particularly large gust of wind caused Pricilla to swerve. The boys had long since stopped their play fighting and sat wide-eyed in their booster seats, taking in the snowy landscape. Streetlights illuminated swirling eddies of snowflakes, spinning like miniature tornadoes before being swallowed up again by the darkness.

Pricilla pulled into the parking lot of Hannaford and shut off the engine. "All right, boys, let's go." Connor and Richard unbuckled their seat belts and piled out of the car after their mother. They immediately grumbled about the cold.

"Hush now," Pricilla said as she hustled them into the store. "We'll be out of the cold soon enough."

Once inside, it was clear they were not the only ones with the same idea. The shelves had been mostly picked clean. Pricilla grabbed what she could, her arms full of canned goods, pasta, and the staple of any blizzard shopping trip: bread and milk. The boys trailed behind her, their little legs struggling to keep up.

"Come on now, we have to hurry," she said as she made her way to the checkout line.

There was only one register open, and no one else seemed to be shopping now. She was the only customer. Pricilla sighed as she got in line, her arms aching from all the cans she was carrying. She glanced down at her boys and smiled as they chattered away to each other, unaware of anything else in the world. Pricilla unloaded her items onto the conveyor belt and looked around. For the first time, she noticed the store appeared to be empty. Just her and her boys. No one else.

"Hello," Pricilla called to the empty store. "Hello?" Her voice echoed down the barren aisles. "Is anyone here?" she called out again, louder this time.

There was no answer but the sound of her boys laughing.

After a few moments of silence, Pricilla heard footsteps from the back, and eventually a lone girl walked toward the register.

"Becky!" Conner screamed as he ran to the gangly red-headed girl. As soon as Richard recognized his favorite babysitter, he ran over as well.

"Hey guys," Becky said with a tense smile. "What are you doing here?"

"Mom had to go shopping for food because scary weather is coming and she has to protect us from it," Connor replied proudly.

"Dad said we are going to make milk sandwiches," Richard said.

Pricilla laughed as she looked at her boys and Becky. Something seemed off with the young girl. Pricilla watched as Becky rang the items up, her hands shivering.

"Are you okay, honey?" Pricilla asked.

Becky looked up at her, and Pricilla was taken aback by the fear in the girl's eyes. "I'm fine," Becky said quickly. "Just hurry and finish up so you can go."

Priscilla glanced at Becky's trembling hands as they moved across the register, quickly scanning their items. "Becky, you're acting like you've seen a ghost. What's wrong? Are you okay?"

Becky looked up, meeting her eyes for just a second before hastily looking away. "I'm fine. You should just check out and leave. Quickly."

Priscilla felt a chill that had nothing to do with the approaching blizzard. She knew when someone was holding back, a skill honed from years of nursing and reading patient expressions. "Becky, if something's wrong, maybe we can help."

Becky's eyes flicked to the store's backroom, then back to Priscilla. Her voice dropped to a hushed tone, tinged with urgency. "Just go, Priscilla. Get your boys and go home. Lock your doors. Don't come back until morning."

Priscilla felt her heart rate quicken. She glanced at Richard and Connor, who were blissfully unaware, arguing softly over a candy bar. She turned back to Becky, her eyes searching for answers. "What aren't you telling me?"

Becky's face tightened, her lips almost quivering. "Please, just trust me. Go now."

And with that, Becky quickly finished scanning their items, bagged them, and almost pushed the cart toward Priscilla. She hesitated for a moment, her instincts screaming that something was dangerously amiss.

Priscilla hesitated, her grip tightening on the cart's handle. She glanced once more at her boys, their innocent faces consumed with the trivial choice of candy. Her eyes then met Becky's, still brimming with that silent, pleading fear. A decision crystallized in her mind.

"No," she finally said, her voice threaded with resolve. "We're not leaving until you tell me what's going on."

Becky looked as if she were about to cry. But before she could say anything, a soft, chilling chuckle emanated from the store's backroom. The sound sliced through the tension like an icy knife.

Becky's face drained of what little color remained.

"It's too late," she whispered, almost inaudible.

The backroom door creaked open, and a man stepped out. Tall and lean, he had a disarming smile that did nothing to reach his icy eyes.

"Ah, a family gathering," he said, his voice dripping with insidious delight. "How heartwarming." He clapped again.

Priscilla felt a chill ripple down her spine. Every fiber in her being screamed to grab her boys and run. Yet, some unseen force rooted her to the spot, as if her feet lead encased her feet.

"Who are you?" she demanded, angling her body protectively in front of Richard and Connor, who seemed to sense the peril and clung to her jeans.

"My name is Jason," he replied, savoring each syllable as if tasting a fine wine. "And you, Priscilla, should have listened to young Becky here." He offered a quick wink to her.

An unnatural calm washed over Priscilla, urging her to nod, to agree, to flee. But her eyes locked onto Becky's, and in that moment, it stripped away all artifice, revealing only raw, naked terror. As Jason circled her like a panther stalking ignorant prey, she kept herself between him and her children.

"Ah, the bravery of mothers. How... intoxicating." Jason's smile widened into a sinister grin, and he sniffed the air as if testing the wind.

"If you're going to do something, know that you'll have to go through me first." Priscilla's heart pounded in her chest, but she held her ground. Jason chuckled again, a sound that made Priscilla's skin crawl.

"Oh, I have no doubt about that, Priscilla. But for now, let's just say... the night is young, and the storm is just beginning." He steps away and beckons to her, "Come. We are having a party in the backroom. I want you, Becky, and your boys to join us."

"No, thank you," Priscilla said, maintaining an ironclad grip on the shopping cart, her knuckles going white. She grabbed at her boys as they took steps towards the stranger. Becky looked back, tears in her eyes as she made her way to the door to the backroom.

"Oh, but I insist," Jason purred, his eyes locking onto hers. A wave of mental energy surged from him, enveloping Priscilla's mind like a suffocating mist.

For a brief moment, she felt her resolve weaken, her grip on the cart loosen. Her body tingled with an inexplicable urge to follow him, as if obeying was the most natural thing in the world. But then her eyes flicked to Connor and Richard. Their faces, masks of youthful bewilderment and worry, snapped her back to reality.

"I said no!" she shouted, her voice tinged with a newfound ferocity.

Jason's eyes narrowed, his smile twisting into a snarl. "You truly are strong-willed, Priscilla. But even you have limits."

A pulse of malignant force emanated from him, striking her willpower like a hammer to a nail. It hurt, as if a physical weight pressed down upon her. She fought it, every cell in her body screaming in defiance, but it was overwhelming.

Reluctantly, agonizingly, she felt her feet move, taking her one step, then another, toward the beckoning darkness of the backroom. Her heart pounded in her chest, dread filling her with each unwilling step.

"Mom? Where are we going?" Connor's voice broke through the heavy air, tinged with panic as the boys began walking with her.

Priscilla tried to answer, to scream, to do anything, but she couldn't. Her voice was a trapped bird within her, fluttering frantically against the bars of Jason's control. And with that, she walked past the register, her children in tow, leaving her shopping and a piece of her soul, as she disappeared into the shadowy abyss of the backroom.

The backroom door swung shut behind them with an ominous creak, sealing off the brightly lit retail space they had just left. Priscilla felt the chill of the room seep into her bones. Fluorescent lights flickered erratically above, casting unsettling shadows that danced on the walls like malevolent spirits.

"What is this place?" Richard whispered, clutching his brother's hand tightly.

Connor's eyes were wide saucers, trying to make sense of the horrors that unfolded before them. The room was in disarray, boxes toppled and goods scattered. But what struck Priscilla the most was the grotesque tableau laid out at the far end of the room.

Becky's coworkers.

Friends and acquaintances of Priscilla.

Their faces twisted in agony with eyes wide open, as their bodies lay across the floor and counters. They looked like marionettes whose strings had been viciously cut. Each one was in a pose, as if frozen in the middle of some desperate, futile action. It was a gruesome mockery of life, a still life painting conceived in Hell.

"Mommy, I'm scared," Connor's voice quivered.

"Stay close to me," Priscilla whispered, her voice laced with a terror she couldn't hide. "Both of you."

"Oh, I'd hoped you'd appreciate my artwork," Jason cooed, stepping out from behind a towering stack of boxes. "It took quite a bit of effort to get them all... cooperative."

Priscilla felt bile rise in her throat. The reality of what Jason had done, the utter debasement of human life, hit her like a sledgehammer.

"You're a monster," she hissed.

Jason chuckled, savoring her revulsion as if it were a fine wine.

"Monster is such a crude term. I prefer to think of myself as an artist. And the human will? Well, that's my canvas."

"Let us go," Priscilla demanded, gathering her boys closer to her, as if she could shield them from the evil that stood before them. "Let us go, or so help me God—"

"Or what? You'll defy me? How did that work out for you last time?" Jason cut her off, his eyes blazing with a malevolent light.

Priscilla's heart was a drumbeat of dread in her chest, but her eyes never wavered from Jason's. She knew she was in a labyrinth of the madman's making, but she also knew she would navigate through hell itself to keep her boys safe.

"What is happening? Who are you?" She pleaded.

Jason leaned against a stack of crates, his eyes locking onto Priscilla's as if trying to peer into her very soul.

"You know, I wasn't always like this. There was a time when I was the epitome of innocence. Just a normal child with a loving family."

Priscilla's heart pounded in her chest as she listened, her instincts screaming at her to find an opening, a weakness, anything.

"That all changed the day my powers emerged," Jason continued, his voice tinged with a faux nostalgia. "Imagine the elation of discovering you can shape the world to your will. It's intoxicating. Imagine you had the ability to make others do things. Things they wouldn't normally do."

Priscilla felt her skin crawl as she clutched her boys closer.

"So, you used your powers to destroy your family. Is that what you're telling me?"

A smirk curled at the edges of Jason's mouth. "Oh, not just destroy. I sculpted them, molded their minds like clay. I orchestrated a masterpiece of psychological horror. You should've seen it, Priscilla. The look in their eyes when they realized they were no longer in control, when they fought against their own hands to keep from killing each other."

Priscilla looked at him with disgust, her body tense, ready to spring into action at the slightest opening. "And you find joy in that, in causing pain?"

"Joy? No, not just joy," Jason said, savoring each word. "Euphoria. The more they resisted, the more delicious their eventual submission. The sensation is... addictive."

Priscilla's eyes flitted from Jason to her boys, then back again. Her mind raced, assembling fragments of plans, contingencies, and desperate ploys. "You're sick, Jason. You need help."

Jason pushed off from the crates and stepped closer, his eyes burning with a perverse intensity. "Oh, I've had help, Priscilla. There's an agency after me. They tried to help. They tried to control me, but all they did was help me understand what I am, and what I'm capable of. And let me tell you, the possibilities are endless."

Jason paced back and forth in front of Priscilla and her boys, his eyes gleaming with a sort of twisted satisfaction. "You might be wondering what brings me to the Bend. I assure you, it's not the weather." As if to drive home his point, the building rattled as the storm intensified.

Priscilla kept her posture rigid, her eyes locked onto Jason's, never betraying the fear that coiled in her gut.

"By all means, enlighten us."

Jason stopped pacing and leaned in, his voice dropping to an almost reverent tone. "Seeds, Priscilla. I've discovered that there are others like me, tiny seeds of potential. And like iron filings to a magnet, we are inexorably drawn to one another."

"More people with abilities like yours," Priscilla muttered, the weight of the revelation settling over her.

"Exactly. But not all seeds deserve to blossom. Most are unworthy, tainted, and would dilute the wonder that is this gift," he said, his eyes narrowing. "So, I've made it my mission to travel across the United States, seeking these seeds out. Snuffing them before they grow into weeds."

"You're killing them," Priscilla said, her voice tinged with revulsion. "You believe that by killing them, you're becoming stronger?"

Jason's eyes gleamed, and for a moment, he looked almost exultant. "Yes, but I'm doing them a favor. Better for me to end them than for them to be found by the agency. Every time I absorb their energy, I become more than what I was. Stronger. Sharper. It's survival of the fittest in its purest form."

Priscilla looked at him, a mix of pity and loathing reflected in her gaze. "You're a monster, Jason. You justify your actions with grandiose theories, but in the end, you're just a killer. Nothing more."

Jason stared back at her, his eyes icy cold, but his lips curling into a smirk. "A monster, perhaps. But a monster who's standing here, relishing his power, while you stand there, powerless to stop me."

Jason paced the room, his steps deliberate, almost ritualistic. "You see, Priscilla, I felt it—the seed—from states away. This one is powerful, unlike anything I've come across. The moment I entered Raven's Bend, it was like being pulled by an invisible string, a magnetic force. We are like two marbles in a spiral. Eventually, we'll collide."

Priscilla held her boys closer, her eyes locked on Jason as he continued.

"A blizzard, of all things, slowed me down," he continued, his voice tinged with a mix of frustration and fascination. "It's as if nature itself is conspiring to protect this seed. It's throwing up a haze that I just can't penetrate. But barriers like that? They're just obstacles to be overcome. I should have found it by now if it weren't for this storm."

Jason paused, turning to face Priscilla and her boys directly, his eyes narrowing. "But rest assured, the storm will stop, the snow will melt, and obstacles will crumble. I will find it, and then it will be just another life extinguished to fuel my evolution."

His words hung heavy in the air, laden with a menace that made Priscilla's skin crawl. She tightened her grip on her sons' hands, her heart pounding with a mixture of fear and resolve.

Jason returned to the table, littered with tools that had dark, twisted purposes. He picked up a pair of gleaming scissors and walked back toward Priscilla.

"Since I have time to kill, so to speak, why not complete my masterpiece?" he said, holding out the scissors toward her. His eyes glittered with malevolent excitement. "You're a nurse, Priscilla. Skilled with your hands, I assume. How would you like to contribute to my art?"

Priscilla stared at the scissors, then back at Jason. Her mind screamed at her to refuse, to run, but she felt that invisible force once again, binding her, shackling her will. It was as though her hands moved of their own accord, slowly reaching out to accept the cold metal handles.

The room seemed to close in on her as she gripped the scissors, Jason's mad grin widening as he watched her struggle against his control.

Priscilla's hand trembled as she took the cold, metal scissors from Jason, feeling an invisible force urging her forward. Her instincts screamed to drop the weapon, to grab her boys and run. Yet, she found herself moving toward Becky; the metal glinting ominously under the dim light of the backroom.

Richard, who had been unusually quiet, suddenly stepped between his mother and Becky. His small face was taut, his eyes locking onto Priscilla's. "Mom, stop," he said, his voice carrying an uncharacteristic weight.

The connection between mother and son acted as an unbreakable tether, pulling Priscilla back from the dark brink where Jason's influence had nearly led her. She felt as if a fog lifted from her mind, clarity replacing confusion. The scissors clattered onto the concrete floor, forgotten.

Jason's eyes narrowed, a subtle snarl escaping his lips. "What just happened?"

It was then that Richard turned his gaze toward Jason. "Leave my family alone," he commanded.

Attempting to flex his mind-controlling muscle, Jason focused intently on Richard, as if he expected the boy to buckle under his will. Instead, he found himself ensnared in a mental tug-of-war he couldn't win, his powers flailing against an unexpected force. The more he pushed, the more he felt himself being pushed back, until he finally stumbled, breaking the psychic connection.

Richard's eyes remained steadfast, a small yet immovable object in the face of an unstoppable force. Jason had found the 'seed' he had been hunting, but it was unlike any he had ever encountered. Something stronger and impossibly resilient.

Realization dawning, Jason staggered back, fear replacing the arrogance on his face. "You're the one," he whispered.

Richard's gaze remained unyielding as he stared into Jason's eyes. "Walk into the storm. Leave us and never return."

Jason clenched his fists, every fiber of his being resisting the command. But Richard's will overpowered him, compelling him forward. With a final, agonizing glance at Priscilla and her boys, Jason turned away, his steps leaden as he walked toward the exit.

He pushed open the door, the frigid gusts of the blizzard engulfing him instantly. Step by step, he moved away from the store, his figure soon becoming indistinct among the swirling eddies of snow. Within moments, he was gone, swallowed by the white-out conditions, as if the storm itself had claimed him.

Richard turned back to his mother, his expression softening. "Mom, let's go home."

Gathering both Richard and Connor to her, Priscilla pulled them close, her arms enfolding them with a desperate urgency that went beyond mere maternal instinct. Her eyes peered through the glass doors to the storm outside, where winds howled and snowflakes danced in a frenzied ballet of gray and white. As she held her sons, their small bodies warm and alive against her own, her thoughts spun into the labyrinth of the future. What had been awakened in Richard tonight? What shadowy paths lay ahead? The weight of these unanswered questions hung heavy in the air, but she knew one thing with unwavering certainty: whatever the future held, they would face it together, an unbreakable bond in an uncertain world.

Around the Bend

"**M**om, are you absolutely certain you can't drive me?" Christopher's voice wavered as he trailed his mother through the immaculate kitchen. The countertops gleamed, a testament to her meticulous nature. Outside, the wind howled, making the windows quiver in their frames as if even the house itself was protesting the blizzard's fury.

His mother paused, her hands hovering over a colander filled with freshly washed vegetables. She shot a quick, almost dismissive glance at the window, then locked eyes with her son. "Chris, you can't be serious. I'm not venturing out in that whiteout, not even for Ash's farewell."

"But it's important, Mom. Ash leaves at dawn, and we won't see him for who knows how long." Christopher sidestepped as his mother pivoted, carrying the colander to the sink. "This is our last chance to say goodbye, all of us together."

She sighed, setting down the vegetables and turning to face him fully. "Look, I get it. But no parent in their right mind would drive in this weather. You'll just have to miss this one, Chris."

Frustration bubbled within him. "Fine," he spat out, storming out of the kitchen.

"Be back in fifteen for dinner!" Her voice trailed after him, a final reminder of the walls closing in as he stomped his way upstairs to his room.

Christopher's footsteps were heavy as he ascended the stairs, each step echoing the weight of his disappointment. He reached his room and closed the door behind him, not with a slam, but with a soft click that felt like a surrender. His room was a sanctuary, a collection of his life's highs and lows—concert posters, a shelf of well-worn books, and photos that captured moments of pure, unfiltered joy.

He sank into his desk chair and stared at the wall, his eyes tracing the outlines of the photos. There was one of him and Ash at Raven's Bend's annual summer music festival, both wearing goofy grins and flower crowns. Ash wore the biggest grin across his pale face. Another showed them on a hiking trip, standing triumphantly at the summit, arms slung around each other. Each image was a pinprick to his heart, a reminder of what he was missing tonight.

His gaze shifted to the old radio on his nightstand. The thought of tuning in to his friends' voices flickered in his mind, but he pushed it away. Not yet, he thought. He wasn't ready to face the bittersweet reality of being there, but not "there."

A sigh escaped his lips as he leaned back, closing his eyes. His thoughts swirled, a mix of frustration, longing, and a sadness he couldn't quite name. It was as if the room itself held its breath, waiting for him to make his next move.

"Christopher, dinner's ready!" His mother's voice broke the silence, pulling him back to the present.

He took a deep breath, steeling himself for the evening ahead. "Coming, Mom," he called back, rising from his chair. As he left his room, he cast one last glance at the radio. Soon, he thought. But not yet.

Christopher descended the stairs and entered the dining room, where the table was set with the meticulous precision only his mother could create, a stark contrast to the tension hanging in the air. His father sat at the head of the table, engrossed in the latest edition of the local paper, The Raven's Bend Journal, while his mother placed a steaming casserole in the center. Stacy, his older sister, was already seated, absently flipping the pages on her recently purchased issue of Teen Beat.

"Sit down, Chris," his mother said, her voice tinged with a forced cheerfulness that did little to lift the mood, "and Stacy, put the magazine down."

As Christopher took his seat, a gust of wind rattled the windows, as if the storm outside wanted to be part of their conversation. His father looked up from his paper and sighed. "This blizzard is really something, huh?" He folded the paper and set it beside his plate.

"Yeah, it's a mess," Christopher replied, his voice flat, his eyes avoiding contact with anyone at the table.

Stacy finally looked up, sensing the tension. "What's eating you, little bro?"

Christopher clenched his fork, contemplating whether to open up. "I was supposed to be at Ash's going-away party tonight. But the 'blizzard of the century' ruined that."

His mother shot him a look, her eyes narrowing. "We've been over this, Christopher. It's not safe to go out."

"I know, Mom. It's just frustrating," he said, his voice rising despite his efforts to keep calm.

His father finally chimed in, setting his paper down. "Life is full of disappointments, son. This is a minor one in the grand scheme of things. Learn this now. When you're young. Better get used to it so when it hits you as an adult, you know what you're dealing with."

Christopher felt a surge of anger but bit his tongue. The room fell silent, save for the sound of silverware clinking against plates and the relentless howling of the wind outside.

As they ate, Christopher's thoughts returned to Ash, to the radio upstairs, and to the words left unsaid. The storm outside mirrored the turmoil he felt within, a tempest of emotions he couldn't quite navigate.

Dinner finally ended, each family member retreating to their own corner of the house, leaving Christopher alone with his thoughts. As he cleared the table, another gust of wind shook the house, as if reminding him that some forces were beyond his control.

Christopher retreated to his room, the tension from dinner still clinging to him like a second skin. He closed the door softly this time, as if hoping to lock out the world and its disappointments. A framed photo on his dresser drew his eyes, a captured moment of pure joy. It was a picture of The Echoes, all six of them, holding a crudely painted wooden sign that bore their self-chosen name.

He picked up the frame, his fingers tracing the contours of their smiling faces. There was Emily, her eyes twinkling with mischief; Jordan, flexing his muscles in mock seriousness; Maya, her smile radiant and knowing; Leo, holding his guitar like a trophy; Ash, his arm casually draped around Christopher's shoulders; and himself, caught in a moment of genuine happiness.

They were The Echoes, a group bound not by popularity or social standing, but by their shared sense of being on the fringes, of not quite fitting into the molds society had set for them. And in that shared experience, they had found a family of sorts, a sanctuary where their voices, often drowned out, could finally be heard.

As he set the photo back down, a gust of wind howled against the windowpane, as if the storm were mocking his sense of loss and isolation. He felt a pang of longing so acute it was almost physical. Tonight, of all nights, he wished he could be with them, to say a proper goodbye to Ash, to share one last adventure as a group before the world pulled them in different directions.

The storm outside raged on, mirroring the tempest of emotions swirling within him. He sank into his bed, clutching a pillow to his chest, as if it could somehow fill the void left by his friends' absence. And for a moment, he allowed himself to be swept away by the memories, each one a fleeting echo of a time when life was simpler, and goodbyes were things that happened to other people.

Summoning a resolve he didn't know he had, Christopher finally turned his gaze to the old radio sitting on his nightstand. It was a relic, but it was their relic, a piece of technology that had somehow become the heartbeat of their friendship. He picked it up, feeling its familiar weight in his hands, and hesitated for a moment before flicking the switch to turn it on.

Static filled the room, a cacophony of white noise that seemed to echo the chaos in his mind. He adjusted the dials, tuning into their designated frequency, the one they had claimed as their own. His heart pounded in his chest as he picked up the microphone, his fingers hovering over the button.

"Echo Five to Echoes, do you copy?" His voice was shaky, tinged with a vulnerability he couldn't hide.

A moment of silence stretched, feeling like an eternity. Then, a crackle broke through the static.

"Echo Two here, is that you, Five?" Ash's voice came through, clear but tinged with surprise.

Relief washed over Christopher. "Yeah, it's me, Echo Five. Mom grounded me because of the storm. I couldn't make it to your place."

"Ah, that's a bummer, man. But hey, you're here now, sort of," Ash replied, a warmth in his voice that made the distance between them feel a little less vast.

"Echo Three checking in," Emily's voice chimed in. "Glad you could join us, Five. I think we are all walled in tonight by the storm."

One by one, the rest of the Echoes checked in—Jordan as Echo Four, Maya as Echo Six, and Leo as Echo One. Each voice was a lifeline, pulling Christopher back from the brink of his own loneliness.

"Echo Five, you still there?" Ash's voice crackled through the radio, pulling Christopher back from his thoughts.

"Yeah, Echo Two, I'm here," Christopher replied, his heart skipping a beat at the sound of Ash's voice.

"So, what's everyone up to? Echo Four, you still working on that jump shot?" Emily chimed in.

"You know it, Three. As soon as my dad and I can clear the driveway, I'm going to be back out there," Jordan responded.

"Echo Six here, buried in a new book as usual," Maya added. "But I could use some company. This blizzard is making me feel like I'm in a Stephen King novel."

Everyone laughed, and Christopher felt a warmth spread through him, as if the miles separating them had suddenly shrunk.

"Echo One, you still strumming away? Got anything for us tonight," Ash asked.

"Always, Two. Working on a new song. I had hoped to have it ready for the party tonight, but I think the snow is giving me a block," Leo responded.

"Can't wait to hear it, man," Ash said, and Christopher could almost see the smile on his face.

"Hey, Echoes, before we get deep into another conversation or we all have to go, I think we should say our goodbyes now," Maya broke in. "Since we can't be there in person, you know?"

"You're right, Six," Emily replied. "Ash, I've been working on a sketch of all of us. I was going to give it to you tonight. I'll mail it instead. And, well, I just want to say you've always been the glue that held us together. We're going to miss you like crazy."

"Thanks, Three. That means the world," Ash responded, his voice tinged with emotion.

"Echo Four here. Ash, I was going to give you my lucky wristband, but I figured you wouldn't want that sweat-stained thing, so I bought you your own lucky band. I'll send it your way.

You've always been the one to push us to be better, man. Keep pushing forward, wherever you go," Jordan added.

"Thanks, Four," Ash said, clearly touched.

"And I've written a song for you, Ash," Leo chimed in. "It's what I'm working on tonight. Sorry, it's not ready yet. I'll record it and send it your way. You've been the melody in the soundtrack of our lives, man. Never stop playing your tune."

"Wow, One, that has to be the cheesiest line I've ever, but I'm honored. And I won't, I promise," Ash replied, his voice softening even more. Everyone chimed in with a good-natured ribbing about Leo's choice of words.

Finally, it was Christopher's turn. He looked at the sealed envelope on his desk, a letter holding words he had never dared to speak aloud. Words confessing how he truly felt about Ash. His heart pounded as he picked up the microphone, his fingers trembling.

"Echo Two, I—uh—I had something special for you. I really wanted to give it to you in person," Christopher stammered, his voice shaky.

There was a pause, and Christopher could almost feel Ash's eyes on him, waiting. "What is it, Five?" Ash finally asked, his voice tinged with curiosity.

"It's—um—it's a letter," Christopher managed to say, avoiding the weight of what the letter actually contained. "I'll mail it to you."

"Thanks, Five. I look forward to reading it," Ash replied, unaware of the emotional turmoil raging within Christopher. "Sorry to cut this short, but my parents are telling me to pack up the radio. We're leaving as soon as the storm clears in the morning," Ash added, injecting a note of finality into the conversation.

Christopher took a deep breath, his finger hovering over the microphone button. This was his moment, his last chance to say what he had always wanted to say. But the words wouldn't come.

"Goodbye, Echo Two. Take care," he finally said, opting for a generic farewell.

"Goodbye, Five. Take care of yourself," Ash responded.

"Goodbye, Echoes. Until next time," Emily chimed in.

"See you when I see you," Jordan added.

"Keep the frequency alive, Echoes," Maya said.

"And keep playing your tunes," Leo concluded.

One by one, the radio fell silent, each friend signing off, leaving Christopher alone in his room. He set the microphone down, his heart sinking. He looked at the letter, then back at the radio. The room was silent now, the static of the radio replaced by the deafening silence of regret. Outside, the storm continued to rage, each gust of wind echoing the missed opportunity, the words left unspoken.

The door creaked open, and Stacy peeked her head in. "Hey, can I come in?" she asked, her voice softer than usual.

Christopher looked up, surprised. "Yeah, sure," he replied, gesturing for her to enter.

Stacy walked in and sat on the edge of his bed, taking in the scene—the radio, the sealed letter, her brother's downcast eyes. "You okay?" she asked, her voice tinged with concern.

Christopher sighed, his shoulders slumping. "Not really. I had a chance to say something important tonight, and I choked."

Stacy looked at the letter on the desk, then back at her brother. "Is that what this is about?" she asked, pointing at the envelope.

"Yeah," Christopher admitted, his voice barely above a whisper.

Stacy reached over and gave her brother's hand a reassuring squeeze. "You know, life gives us second chances, but sometimes we have to create them ourselves."

Christopher looked up, meeting his sister's eyes. "You think so?"

"I know so," Stacy replied, her voice filled with a conviction he found comforting. "And hey, storms don't last forever. Neither do missed opportunities."

For the first time that night, Christopher felt a glimmer of hope, a sense that maybe, just maybe, he could find the courage to say what he had left unsaid. Outside, the storm continued its relentless assault, but inside, the atmosphere felt a little less heavy.

Christopher sat alone in his room, the letter still unopened on his desk. He stared out the window, watching as the storm continued its relentless dance, each snowflake a fleeting moment, each gust of wind a missed opportunity. Time seemed to stretch and bend, the minutes blurring into hours; the night deepening around him.

His eyes flicked to the clock. It was nearing the predawn hours, that quiet time when the world holds its breath before the break of a new day. An idea formed in his mind, a spark of inspiration fueled by the weight of his regrets and the ticking of the clock.

He looked at the letter one last time, then made up his mind. Rising from his chair, he moved to his closet and geared up for the Maine winter. He pulled on thermal socks, laced up his heavy boots, and donned a pair of insulated pants. Next came a thermal shirt, a heavy sweater, and his thickest down jacket. He found his gloves, hat, and a scarf, wrapping himself in layers as if armoring against the cold—and his own vulnerability.

With the letter tucked securely into an inner pocket, he headed downstairs, careful not to wake his family. The house was silent, as if granting him this moment, this chance to reclaim what had been lost. He scratched a quick note for his parents letting them know where he would be and for them not to worry about him.

Outside, the storm had finally relented, the snowfall easing, the wind dying down to a whisper. It was as if the world itself were granting him passage, a brief respite in the tempest of his emotions. Christopher stepped out into the predawn light, his footsteps crunching in the freshly fallen snow.

His destination was clear: Ash's house. It was a long walk, especially in the snow, but each step felt like a small victory, a reclaiming of the words left unspoken, and the feelings left unshared.

Christopher trudged through the snow, his boots crunching with each step. The cold was biting, but determination fueled him, warming him from within. Soon, he reached his first waypoint: Jordan's house. It was still dark, the windows like blank eyes staring out into the night.

He scooped up a handful of snow, squeezing it into a ball. Taking aim, he threw it at Jordan's window. Once, twice, three times. On the fourth throw, he saw a light flicker on, and then Jordan's face appeared behind the glass.

Their eyes met, and in that instant, neither needed words. Jordan's eyes widened in recognition, then narrowed in understanding. He gave a quick nod, a silent agreement passing between them.

Christopher watched as Jordan disappeared from the window, only to reappear a few minutes later, fully dressed and geared up for the winter chill. The front door opened, and Jordan stepped out, locking eyes with Christopher once more.

"Ready?" Christopher asked, though the question was almost unnecessary.

"Let's do this," Jordan replied, his voice tinged with a resolve that mirrored Christopher's own.

Together, they set off into the predawn light, two friends bound by a shared mission, a shared history, and a shared understanding that some things in life are too important to be left unsaid.

With Jordan by his side, Christopher felt a renewed sense of purpose. They made their way to Emily's house next, then Maya's, and finally Leo's. At each stop, the ritual was the same: a snowball at the window, a flicker of light, and a face appearing in the glass. Each time, recognition was followed by understanding, a nod, and then the friend would reappear, geared up and ready to face the winter's chill.

By the time they reached Leo's house, the first hints of dawn were painting the sky in shades of soft pink and orange. They were now a group of five, each one silently committed to this unspoken mission, each one understanding the weight of the moment and the words left unsaid.

As they rounded the final bend, Ash's house came into view. The sky was now awash in the soft light of dawn, casting long shadows on the snow-covered ground. Christopher felt his heart leap into his throat as he saw the scene unfolding before them: Ash's family was loading suitcases into the car, the engine already running, exhaust fumes mixing with the crisp winter air.

The five friends exchanged glances, their faces etched with a mix of relief and apprehension. Without a word, they quickened their pace, their boots crunching in the snow as they closed the distance.

Ash was at the trunk of the car, his back turned to them as he arranged the last of the luggage. His father was in the driver's seat, and his mother was holding the car door open, her eyes scanning the horizon as if expecting someone.

And then she saw them. Her eyes widened in surprise, then softened in understanding. She said something to Ash, who turned around, his eyes following his mother's gaze.

The moment their eyes met, Christopher felt a rush of emotions flood over him—relief, joy, but also a pang of regret for the words still trapped inside him. Ash's face broke into a wide smile, and he left the luggage to run toward them.

"Guys, what are you doing here?" Ash exclaimed as he reached them, his eyes shining with disbelief and happiness.

Christopher stepped forward, the letter still tucked in his pocket, its weight both a burden and a promise. "We couldn't let you leave without a proper goodbye," he said, his voice steady for the first time that night.

Ash looked at each of his friends, his eyes lingering on Christopher for a moment longer than the rest. Then, as if pulled by an invisible force, they all stepped in for a group hug, arms wrapping around each other, faces pressed close. For a few seconds, the world outside ceased to exist; it was just them, the Echoes, bound by friendship and a shared history that no distance could erase.

As they finally broke the embrace, Ash stepped back, his eyes shining. "I can't believe you guys did this," he said, his voice thick with emotion.

"We had to," Emily replied, her own eyes misty.

"Yeah, man, we couldn't let you go without a proper send-off," Jordan added, his voice tinged with a warmth that cut through the winter chill.

Christopher felt Ash's eyes on him again, and this time, he met the gaze squarely, the unsaid words hanging heavy between them but softened by the depth of their friendship.

From the car, Ash's parents watched the scene unfold, their faces etched with a mixture of surprise and deep emotion. Ash's mother wiped away a tear, and his father gave a nod, as if acknowledging that some friendships are so strong, they can weather any storm.

Ash's eyes flicked to Christopher's. "What about the letter you mentioned? Did you bring it?"

Christopher hesitated, his eyes meeting Ash's. "I—I forgot it," he stammered, the lie slipping out before he could stop it.

Ash looked at him, a mix of disappointment and curiosity in his eyes. "What did it say?"

Christopher opened his mouth to speak, but the words wouldn't come. Instead, he mumbled something about friendship and memories, avoiding Ash's gaze.

From beside him, Emily gave him a sharp elbow to the ribs, her eyes meeting his in a look that said, "Tell the truth."

And there it was, the moment hanging between them, heavy with the weight of unsaid words and unspoken feelings.

Christopher looked at Emily, his eyes wide with surprise. "You know? How?"

The group erupted into laughter, the tension momentarily broken.

"Come on, dude," Jordan chimed in, grinning from ear to ear. "It's the worst-kept secret among the Echoes. The only ones who don't seem to know are you and Ash."

The laughter continued, but Christopher felt his cheeks flush, a mix of embarrassment and relief washing over him. For a moment, he locked eyes with Ash, who looked equally surprised and intrigued.

Christopher took a deep breath, his eyes meeting Ash's. "Look, Ash, the letter was—well, it was more than just about friendship and memories. It was a confession. I've had feelings for you for a long time now." He paused, his heart pounding in his chest. "But I've been scared, you know? Scared of how you'd react, scared of what this distance would do to us, and most of all, scared that I'd ruin the incredible friendship we have."

The words hung in the air, heavy but liberating, as Christopher looked at Ash, waiting for a response, his heart both hopeful and fearful.

Ash looked at Christopher, his eyes searching, then softening. "Chris, you should've told me sooner. Not just for your sake, but for mine, too. I've been carrying around the same feelings, and the same fears, for a long time now." He paused, taking a step closer. "Friendship like ours isn't so easily ruined. And distance is just geography. Feelings? They're a lot harder to map out, but they're also a lot harder to shake. I'm really glad you told me, Chris. Because now, I can tell you—I feel the same way."

As Ash's words settled in, Christopher felt a warmth spread through him, as if a weight had been lifted, replaced by something far more exhilarating. For the first time in what felt like forever, he felt seen, understood, and, most importantly, reciprocated.

As Christopher and Ash shared a moment of mutual understanding, Maya piped up from the background, her voice tinged with amusement. "Well, it's about time you two figured it out. We've all been placing bets on when you'd finally come clean."

The group erupted into another bout of laughter, the tension of the moment dissolving into the easy camaraderie that had always defined them.

"Wait, you were betting on us?" Christopher asked, his eyes widening in mock indignation.

"Let's just say some of us are going to be collecting big time," Jordan replied, grinning from ear to ear.

The laughter continued, but for Christopher and Ash, the weight of unspoken words had been lifted, replaced by the comforting presence of their friends and the exhilarating promise of something new.

As the laughter died down, Ash's mother approached the group, her eyes misty but her smile warm. "We really need to get going, Ash."

Ash nodded, his eyes meeting each of his friends before settling on Christopher. "I guess this is it, then."

"Yeah, for now," Christopher replied, his voice tinged with a newfound optimism.

Ash moved in for one final group hug, his arms wrapping around his friends as if trying to hold on to the moment just a little longer. "Take care, Echoes," he said, his voice thick with emotion.

"We will, Echo Two. You better keep that radio handy," Emily responded, her own voice catching.

With a final wave, Ash turned and climbed into the car. As the engine revved, he looked out the window, locking eyes one last time with Christopher. No words needed; their expressions said it all.

The car pulled away, its tires crunching over the frosty snow on the freshly plowed road, gradually disappearing around the bend. And as it did, Christopher felt a mix of sadness and hope, a sense of an ending but also a beginning, the closing of one chapter, and the tentative turning of one page in another.

Down From the Mountain

The patrons of the Great Falls Tavern ignored the storm beating against the windows. The wind and snow raged against the walls, buffeting the building in the icy blasts of the Nor'easter brewing outside. The streetlights, barely visible in the storm, cast their sickly yellow light across the street. A lone plow truck rumbled past, only the cab and driver visible above the immense plowline. It grated against the road as it piled the snow even higher. The aging bartender, Keith Davidson, looked at the clock, then at the muted television displaying updated weather alerts. He sighed and tugged the hem of his white tee-shirt as he rapped his hand twice on the counter, gaining the attention of most of the remaining patrons.

"A'right, folks," he said, raising his voice above the wind raging against the building, "last call. You need to git before you're snowed in here. I ain't babysitting the lot of ya tonight. Maine's finest have just cleared the roads for you sorry lot." A few groans of protest greeted his announcement. He responded to one regular in particular, "Sammy, quit your bellyaching. Mary will be waiting for you. Weather says it's just going to get worse and I'm not having you sleep here tonight. Go on." He swiped the wad of cash in front of Sam and patted his regular on the shoulder.

Out of the six left in the bar, all but one shuffled outdoors, bracing themselves against the biting wind as it whipped in through the open door. The lone patron left remained seated at the bar, sipping his drink, as he had all night. Except for his original order, there were no words from the newcomer the entire night as he sat at the bar. He just continued to sip the drink slowly, his mouth obscured by the long black hair hanging around his face. Keith sized him up. Below the hair hanging in front of his eyes, Keith saw the high cheekbones and dark complexion of the local tribe of Native Americans who occasionally wandered into town from the reservation. The bartender considered the stranger's thin wiry frame beneath his tattered brown trench coat. He reached for the baseball bat he kept behind the bar as he waved at his departing regulars. Keith approached the stranger and leaned low to look into the man's face. He swallowed hard and tapped the bar top in front of the stranger's glass.

"Time to go, sir. It's time for me to be closing. Time to pay up." The stranger laughed and sipped his drink again. When he set it down, Keith gently pulled the glass away and said, "You need to leave before the storm outside gets worse. Weather says if you don't head out now, it'll be rough going home. Now's a good enough time." As the stranger laughed again, parting his hair from his face with his forefinger, Keith received his first good look at the man's face. The gray eyes that stared out from a smooth, young face carried a weight, an age to them.

"How's a deal sound?" The stranger said, his voice low and gentle. "A wager. A gamble. If I win, I'll not pay, and you'll let me weather the storm here for the night."

"Are you crazy? You need to leave." Keith gripped the bat tighter in his hand and stood upright.

Before the stranger could respond, the wind howled as the door opened to the maelstrom outside. A large man bundled in multiple layers of furs ducked to enter the bar. He shook his body, knocking the accumulated snow onto the floor in the opening, then turned and pushed the door shut against the wind. He took three large strides and set himself on the stool two down from the stranger. He did not speak, but sat staring at the other two men. Keith glanced at the stranger, who took his glass back and returned to his drink.

"I'm sorry, sir, but we're closed. I just haven't locked the door yet."

"No, I think I'll be staying," the larger man said, his voice boomed throughout the bar. "I have business to discuss with your customer." He pulled his hood back and revealed a face set deep within a shaggy black beard.

"Nothing to discuss with me," the stranger said above his drink. He took another sip and continued, "You interrupted us. I was about to wager with our fair purveyor of whiskey."

The larger of the two snorted.

"Azeban, you still trying to swindle free stuff from them? From what I hear, you're not even good at it anymore."

"Now, gentlemen, I must insist," Keith slammed his hand down on the countertop, "the two of you leave now or I'll..."

"You'll do what?" The larger man stood and continued, "No police are coming out in this storm. You don't have a weapon that could hurt the two of us. You'll do nothing." He leaned forward, his face shimmering in the dim light, and his features became blurry. He inhaled deeply, and large white feathered wings rose behind him and his face appeared covered in feathers. The storm increased in intensity, and the building shook. Keith backed into the shelf and knocked bottles onto the floor. He slipped on the spilled liquor, but caught his balance before he fell. Regaining his footing, he ran for the front door and out into the storm, his screams lost in the wind. The winged man shifted back to his original appearance, walked over and shut the door, and said, "Now, Azeban, we need to talk."

"Bemola, first you need to calm the storm before you kill that poor man. Then, we'll talk." Bemola waved his hand, and the storm reduced its intensity. Azeban continued, "Why are you here? Did Dabaldak send you? Does the Great One want you to bring the raccoon back to the family?" He twirled his hand and bowed his head toward Bemola.

"Raccoon," Bemola said as he laughed, and continued, "you haven't assumed that shape in about a hundred years from what I hear. But no, to answer your question, Dabaldak didn't send me. You know the Great One doesn't really get involved in family matters for the most part." He paused and bobbed his head from one side to the other before saying, "No, Gluskab sent me."

"What?" Azeban stood, the stool falling behind him, the clattering echoing in the empty bar. "Gluskab knows how I feel about him. Why do you think I've been with the humans all these years? He lied to us." He slammed his fist down, cracking the thick wood of the bar, and said, "More importantly, he lied to them. He told them he would come back, but he never did. Why does he want me now?"

"You're right, Aze." Bemola leaned over the bar and grabbed a bottle at random. He twisted the cap and pulled the bottle to his lips. Before taking a drink, he said, "He didn't come back, but that doesn't mean that he won't." The bottle upended into his mouth. After a long draught of the alcohol, he sighed and continued, "That's what he's planning. He promised the People of the Dawnlands that he would return, and that is just what he is doing now. He is gathering the family back together and we will be with him when he returns to the People."

"Bemola, you've got to be kidding me?" Azeban straightened his stool and sat back at the bar. He put his finger on the larger man's chest and said, "You've been on Katahdin for far too long. You haven't seen what's been happening to the People. You don't know what they've been through. It would have been better for them had Gluskab never shown them the way. We should have never interfered."

"He thinks that now that they are regrouping and growing again, it is time to return."

"He wants to come back," Azeban spat on the bar between the two men and continued, "as the benevolent hero and lead them to a glorious return. Snow Bird, go back to your mountain and make storms." Azeban waved his hand at Bemola as he leaned over the bar and returned to his drink.

"Do you not care for the family?" Bemola said as he rose from his seat. A hint of feathers showed on his face as he said, "Whatever your differences with Gluskab, the fact remains that we need you." His face blended back to human features as he took a step away from Azeban.

"What are you not telling me, old friend? What can I do that Gluskab cannot?" Azeban placed his glass down and met Bemola's gaze.

"It's Miko. He's never forgiven Gluskab for turning him into a squirrel."

"That was pretty funny," Azeban said between laughs, "but what does that have to do with me?"

"You and Miko were close. You were the tricksters." Bemola took another pull from his bottle.

"Yes, but I never condoned when he killed and ate humans. He and I never saw eye to eye on that. It wasn't until he was changed that we," Azeban wavered his hands back and forth, "worked together. I wouldn't say we were friends, but we trusted each other."

"That is why Gluskab wants you. Miko has vowed to not allow Gluskab to return. Not just that, but he has promised to use all his powers to terrorize the People."

"What's he going to do as a squirrel? Bite their ankles?" Azeban tilted his head to the side and raised an eyebrow.

"No, as the ages have passed, he has been able to shift his form, as you and I can. Gluskab's powers keep him from returning to his form as a wolf or bear, as of now he can only be a squirrel or a human," Bemola leaned closer to Azeban and lowered his voice, "but he is working to undermine the People as a human would. He fights against them and against us. He is no longer just a simple trickster anymore. As time passes, he is closer to returning to full power. We need you to talk to him and if he won't listen, we need you to stop him."

"Why? The People are fine without Gluskab. If he comes back now, it will not be what he expects."

Bemola placed his hands on Azeban's shoulders and said, "Don't do this for Gluskab. Do it for the People of the Dawnlands. Miko's true nature has been suppressed by his form for so long. You know what he will be like when he regains his old habits. You are the only one in the family that he will talk to."

Azeban pressed the bridge of his nose between his fingers, breathed deep, and muttered under his breath. "You mean that I'm the only one that he will allow to get close enough. Bemola," he said as he stepped away, "go back to your mountain. Keep making your storms. Stay away from the humans you claim to care about so much. They don't need us anymore. Tell Gluskab that if he wants to come back, to do so quietly. Live amongst the People of the Dawn as one of them. They need us to learn who they are, serve them, not to come back and lead them as lords above. I know Gluskab wants to come back and do as he did once before. Gift them knowledge and protect them, but he has not returned for so long. How would they feel? Would they feel as I do?" Azeban paced as he said, "That he did not come back in their time of need. I don't know, but I do know that we need to stay out of their lives." He stopped and held his hand outstretched to Bemola as he continued, "So, go back to your mountain. Send word to the family that I am not returning. I will find Miko and will try to reason with him. It may take a trickster to capture a trickster." Bemola opened his mouth to speak but Azeban continued, "No. I'm not coming back. Gluskab can come after me himself if he wants, but it's not up for debate. Now if you'll excuse me, I'll be going."

Bemola reached out to grasp Azeban, but his fingers passed through the trickster, leaving ripples in the image as if his body were made of water. He shook his head. The storm grew louder, and the blizzard grew to a whiteout condition.

"How long have you been gone, my friend?" His voice echoed in the bar and the wind blasted with every syllable.

"Just during my last speech to you," the image of Azeban said. "Sorry to have fooled you, brother." He paused and allowed himself a half-smile before continuing, "Oh, actually, not really, I couldn't stay and have you take me home. I may be a trickster, but you are far stronger than I. Please tell Gluskab to not interfere. Tell him, no, tell all of them to come live among the people. Our age is done. Let's live as they do. On the ground amongst them and not in the sky over them. We had a good run. Go back to your mountain. Maybe I'll see you next time you come down."

The image faded as it walked away, and Bemola stood alone in the deserted bar. He laughed and shook his head again before walking out into the storm. As the snow and wind tore at him, he raised his arms to the sky and let the Nor'easter carry him back to his mountain. Above the roar of the storm, the screech of an owl faded away on the wind.

One Mile Home

The warehouse rumbled against the Nor'easter raging outside. The steel frame shuddered against the icy blast. David locked up his office and walked down the hallway, muttering a silent thanks to the inventor of the automatic start on his SUV. He placed his laptop case and lunch box on the counter at the security office and turned to the "In/Out" board for management. He flicked his tab, "David Allen- Security Manager" from "In" to "Out," and turned back to the office where the security officer, Nancy, peeked into his bags.

"Cold night out, David," she said as she glanced in his case and box, "you drive safe on the way home. It going to be a rough one, I hear." She pushed his belongings toward his side of the counter and leaned out, glancing at the white fury blowing right outside the front doors.

"I'll be fine, don't you worry. I live just across the river. You all be safe tonight. Don't do your rounds until this wind dies down." David turned to the door, then paused. He took a step back and said, "Hand me the phone, and hit the extension for the Gate, please." Nancy removed the phone from the receiver and handed it to him. She pressed the button labeled "Truck Gate," and the line trilled in his ear.

"Truck Gate, Mike speaking," David heard.

Mike, David here," he leaned his head through the window into the security office and looked at the monitor bank on the far wall, most of them just showing blowing snow, "you stay inside up there unless absolutely necessary. Use as much salt as you need and make sure they plow up there. I don't want any trucks sliding into the building. You hear me?"

"No worries, boss. I'm not green. I know what I'm doing."

"I know. Just be safe out there tonight. It's a bad one."

"Goodnight, boss." Mike laughed before hanging up the line. David handed the phone back to Nancy with a nod.

"Get you outta here before it gets much worse," Nancy said as she returned the phone to the receiver. "Give that little girl of yours a hug for me, won't ya?"

"You bet. I'll see you tomorrow." David grabbed his case and lunch box.

"Nope, you won't. I'm taking vacation tomorrow. Taking my granddaughter to some new movie at that theater over in Topsham, so I took the night off."

"Oh, that's right. Sorry about that."

"No problem. I'm just a second shift grunt. How can I expect the bosses to keep up with my comings and goings?" She smiled and winked at David as he placed his hand on the door.

"You know better than that," he retorted. "Enjoy the movie tomorrow. Hope you have a blast." He paused as he opened the door. "Call me if anything weird happens tonight, won't you?"

"Of course, boss. Go home. Rest up," she leaned to look out at the storm again and continued, "You'll need it to dig outta this one. Weather says we've already gotten two-and-a-half feet, with more on the way. Oh, and next time we have a big storm, you might want to wear your snow pants." She pointed at his jeans and clucked her tongue.

"Don't worry about me. You guys just stay warm and safe tonight. I'm just going to my car. I'll be fine."

David smiled as he pulled a facemask over his head, zipped up his jacket, and pushed his way out of the entryway. The wind fought against the door as he slipped outside into the frigid blasting wind. He squinted his eyes as the icy wind stung them.

He used his knees to break the snow as he trudged through the unplowed portion of the parking lot toward his SUV. At the far end of the lot, the yellow flashing lights from the snowplow are all he could see of the monstrous piece of equipment. David reached his vehicle and opened the back hatch. Setting his bag and lunch box down, he picked up a brush and a small snow shovel.

He worked with haste to clear the vehicle, brushing off the elbow-deep snow from the top of the car before moving down to the windshield and hood. The wind roared by, stinging his eyes with blasts of snow and ice. By the time he finished, a half inch had accumulated over his car. After tossing the brush into the backseat, David waded through the snow to the back of the SUV. He dug massive heaps of the snow away from the back tires and used his body to knock down the plow line, walling his vehicle into the spot. He stopped after tossing the last shovel of snow away from his car and leaned on the shovel, huffing loudly. Large puffs of vapor escaped his mouth, only to be swept away by the howling wind.

David opened the back hatch of his SUV and tossed the shovel inside. It landed with a thud and knocked snow over the gray carpet of the interior. He paused before getting in the car as the plow roared up behind his car and stopped. Peter, the driver, decked out head to toe in an orange snow suit, hopped out and ran over to David.

"Everything okay, Pete?" David shouted over the wind.

"You sure you want to be heading out in this? I hear the roads are rough." Pete pulled down his facemask and continued, "It's bad out there."

"I know," David chuckled, "but I'll be damned if I'm sleeping in the warehouse tonight. Weather like this is what four-wheel drive is for."

"I hear 'ya. I hear 'ya." Peter turned back to his plow and waved his hand. "If your mind is made up, then follow me out to the road. I can at least make sure you can make it out of the parking lot."

"Thanks, Pete. Much appreciated." David spun on his heel and walked to the driver's side door. Already warm and ready to go. He took a moment to get comfortable, taking off his heavy coat, gloves, hat, and face mask. He set them in the passenger seat and aimed a heater vent down toward his wet gear. David buckled his seat belt and backed out of the spot. After spinning the tires for a second, he finally managed to gain traction and pull away.

The heavy white flakes buffeted against the windshield as David pulled right onto the main road. His headlights illuminated only a few car lengths ahead of the bumper. David squinted as he followed the road, more by memory than by being able to see the asphalt beneath the thick covering of snow. Peering out his passenger window, he saw the Nor'easter swallow up the bright lights of the warehouse that usually illuminated the sky for miles around. He looked back to the road and leaned forward, his forehead close to the glass; close enough that David felt the cold wicking heat from his head.

He continued through town past the abandoned mill buildings, relics of the past glory of Raven's Bend, Maine. The frames of the old buildings outlined in the deepening snow blended into the white of the storm as he drove past. A plow rumbled past, and David felt the vibrations in his feet. He continued at a snail's pace, keeping his head forward and eyes focused. He slowed to a stop at the light before the green bridge that leads to the rural outskirts of the town and toward home. The blinker clicked in time with the wiper blades as he waited for the light to turn. The tires spun again as he pulled forward and left at the light. On the bridge, he felt the wind pushing the side of the vehicle and he fought to keep in a straight line.

Once over the bridge, David turned left again, past the Rollerdrome, lot empty, lights off; no loitering teens waiting for their parents to pick them up on a night like tonight. David knew the river ran just to the left of the road, but with the visibility, there was no indication of the waters of the Androscoggin flowing beyond the white. He kept driving and the faint lights of the town disappeared into the blizzard, replaced with the dim outlines of pines briefly showing through the whiteout, only to fade away as well. No other cars traveled the road along the river. David gripped the wheel as the vehicle pushed through the thick snow and feathered the gas pedal as he rolled into the rural section of Raven's Bend.

After fifteen minutes of driving at ten miles per hour, David finally came to his road. He took care as he turned right to stay away from where he assumed the shoulder lay beneath the accumulated snow. He eased back into a straight line after the car slid coming out of the turn. David's knuckles whitened as he gripped the wheel. Coming down the hill, he picked up speed to help him on the next incline. His car slowed on the uphill but managed to make it to the top.

"Damn it," he exclaimed as his headlights illuminated the snow drifting onto the road from the open field to his right. The drift made his lane undrivable. Four feet of snow crept into the road and seeped across the middle of the road. The wind tore through the farmland unburdened. The blinding snow flew horizontally past the windshield. David slowed to a stop, then pulled into the opposite lane. He eased forward as the wind whipped around his SUV. He turned the wheel slightly to the right as he felt the car pulling with the blasts of wind. He looked at the GPS on the dash.

"One mile home. Not too much farther."

He felt the plow vibrating his car before he saw the headlights. That brief advanced notice allowed him to jerk the wheel to the right. His car plowed deep into the drift, burying the hood into the snow as the plow sped past him on the left. As the vehicle dove into the deep snow, the engine sputtered to a stop.

Shaking, he sat gulping down deep breaths of air and flexing his fingers. In the rear-view mirror, the plow disappeared into the muted white of the storm. David turned the key in the ignition. The dash lights lit up, but the engine did not start. He tried three more times, to no avail. David closed his eyes and took a few deep breaths, flexing his fingers as he breathed.

"Please, start," he said, with his eyes still closed.

He turned the key.

Nothing.

"Damn it." David slapped his hands down hard on the steering wheel. He leaned over to the passenger seat, retrieved his coat, and dug through the pockets to retrieve his phone. David long pressed the number two, and the display read "Dialing Home." After six rings, the answering machine came on.

"Hi," his wife's voice said over the phone speaker, "You've reached Abigail and David Allen. Please leave a message after the beep." David rubbed his forehead as the shrilling beep screamed at him from his phone.

"Babe, I'm down the road from home and buried the car in a snowdrift. I'm about a mile from the house. I know I was supposed to be working until the morning, but I was able to leave early. Call me when you get this." He hung up the phone and placed it on the dash. He drummed lightly on the steering wheel while watching his phone.

"Call me." He drummed a little faster. "Come on, honey, call me back."

The phone remained silent as the only audible sound came from the howling wind and pattering of snow striking the windshield. David struck the steering wheel as hard as he could.

"Damn it, I can't believe I did this." He shook his head and tried his house one more time on his phone. When the answering machine picked up, he immediately hung up and tossed his phone onto the passenger seat. "Damn it." He rested his forehead against the steering wheel as the wind whipped around the vehicle, already drifting the snow over the hood and up onto the windshield.

David checked his phone again and pulled his coat into his lap. He clenched it close to his body before inserting his arms into the sleeves. Zipping the coat, he let loose another swear, then pulled his knit cap over his head and exited the vehicle.

The wind and snow whipped around his face, stinging his eyes. The wind ripped the door from his hands, slamming it shut. David looked up and down the road, squinting to see the plow, but visibility remained low. He turned toward home and waded through the waist high snow to where it only came up to his calf.

"Only one mile to go," David whispered.

He pulled his facemask over his mouth and tightened his hood around his head as he began the trek through the maelstrom. He trudged through the thick blanket of snow as the storm intensified. David searched with the tip of his boot until he found the edge of the road and tried to keep his feet along the crumbling asphalt buried beneath the snow. He meticulously placed one foot in front of the other as pushed through the snow and against the wind.

"One, two, three," David counted his steps, trying to keep track of his progress. He looked back to see how far away from his SUV he had walked, only to see the white wall of snow blowing sideways. Looking back in the direction he needed to go, David continued his trek. The wind shifted, and he fought to stay upright, flailing his arms to maintain his balance. David's eyes stung from the assault of ice and snow pelting his face. He held one hand in front of his eyes as he walked.

David lost sense of time and distance as he stumbled in his count. He fumbled in his pocket and brought out his phone. It lit up, but before he could check the time, it slipped out of his gloved hand, falling into the deep snow.

"Shit," dropping to his knees, he fumbled around in the drift, searching for any sign of his cell. He took off his gloves and set them on the drift, then dove back into the snow. A low vibration in the snow, different from the wind, gave him a pause. The vibration grew more intense. David felt it rattling his feet and into his legs. Looking up, he saw the plow barreling down the road toward him, the driver oblivious to David's plight. David dove to the right, just as the plow roared past like an angry beast chewing through the snow. The cascade of snow thrown from the plow washed over David like an ocean wave, burying him beneath feet of heavy snow. David slowly crawled his way back onto the freshly plowed road, shouting in vain at the fading taillights of the snowplow.

He turned and looked at the path of the road, freshly plowed, and he breathed a sigh of relief. He stuck his bare hands deep into his pockets and waked toward home.

David felt the cold leaching the heat from his body. Snow stuck to his eyebrows and lashes. His facemask frosted over from the vapor of his exhaled air. As he pushed onward, his limbs grew heavy and his footfalls plodded along the road. David noticed the snow thickening on the road as the wind drifted it down and across the open fields. The recently cleared path of the plow disappeared as the storm reclaimed the road. David kept shuffling forward, trying to keep his foot on the pavement. His visible path forward vanished into the storm. His heart skipped, and his stomach turned as he lost the sensation of walking on the asphalt.

"No, no, no!" David screamed as he kicked his feet around in the snow. He searched in vain for the hard edge of the road, but only felt the crunch of snow and ice beneath his feet. He twirled around, looking into the gray-white swirling around him. David fell to his knees and let the wind buffet him.

"Come on, it was only one mile," David shouted into the storm.

He stood and squared himself off against the wind. Picking a direction, he set off into the snow. Into the storm.

The fuzzy static of the Nor'easter swallowed him up, and he disappeared.

In the morning, the wind had finally died down, and the sun blasted bright upon the blanket of snow left from the storm the night before. A silence permeated the fields, only broken by the whispers of snow falling from the boughs of the pines. One mile from David's home, his red SUV remained buried deep within the drifting snow, blinkers still ticking along in a slow rhythm. All traces of David's trek the night before had been blown away during the storm. No footprints, no swath cut through the snow, no sign of his passage told the tale.

The only trace left of David's walk lay within sight of his house; an old white farmhouse framed against the morning sky with smoke gently pouring from the chimney. At the edge of David's property, near the barbed fence of the neighboring cattle field, a piece of blue fabric, the sleeve of David's coat, flapped in the wind. The wind pulled back the sleeve to expose David's blue icy hand as he lay entombed beneath the hard-packed snow.

THE PLOW

R aven's Bend slumbered beneath a downy quilt of snow, an ivory world where the natural and the man-made blended into a frozen tableau. A Nor'easter had rolled in, its icy breath kissing the rooftops and frosting the trees in sparkling attire. The town was hushed, save for the muted rumble of an approaching snowplow.

Tim gripped the worn steering wheel, his knuckles pale against the grime that had accumulated over the years. The cab smelled of motor oil and stale beer, a mix that had long become his refuge against the loneliness. His radio crackled with the soft voice of a country singer lamenting love lost—yet another bottle poured down the sink of heartache.

In the center console, a flask of whiskey lay beside a crumpled pack of cigarettes. Tim had struggled with the bottle for years, and tonight, the temptation was as thick as the snowflakes outside. He shook his head, trying to scatter the thought like so many snowflakes in the wind.

The plow's blade grumbled as it ate through the snow, pushing it aside to clear a path for tomorrow's travel. The act was mechanical, rhythmic, allowing Tim's mind to drift. He thought of his estranged daughter, her voice a distant echo in his memories. He wondered if she would be home for Christmas this year, though deep down, he knew the answer.

And then, in a blink, it happened. A thud, the kind of sound that turns the gut to ice and snaps a drifting mind into cruel focus.

Tim's heart thundered in his chest, each beat a deafening drum against the backdrop of the Nor'easter's wail. Slowly, he unlatched the door and stepped out into the storm. The world was a swirl of white, as if heaven and earth were blending into a single, snowy tapestry. Wind gusted, lashing his face with icy tendrils and cutting through his coat like shards of glass.

His boots crunched in the fresh snow as he trudged to the front of the plow. Each step felt like an eternity, each footfall a muffled drumroll leading up to a grim crescendo.

"Please, God, let it be a deer," he murmured through chattering teeth, his breath frosting in the frigid air.

And then he saw it.

A figure.

A prone figure sprawled awkwardly on the ground. It was not a deer. No, this was unmistakably human. A man in a black suit and tie lay before him, his body angled in a way that defied life. His skin was ashen, a stark contrast to the suit he wore, as if the color had been drained from him by the cold or something far worse.

For a moment, Tim's world narrowed to this tragic spectacle: the stranger's pallid face framed by swirling snowflakes, the chilling wind that seemed to carry a note of accusation, the biting cold penetrating through his layers, reaching into his very soul.

His flask of whiskey called to him from the cab of the plow, but for once, the urge to drown his troubles seemed a distant concern. Here, in the eye of the storm, with a life extinguished, Tim knew he was at a crossroads.

Tim stood there, snowflakes settling on his shoulders like ethereal witnesses, his mind a tempest of conflicting thoughts. The law dictated one course of action, but self-preservation whispered another. He was an old man, haunted by a past steeped in regret and amber liquid. Could he afford another blemish on his already tarnished life?

The wind howled, as if urging him to decide. His eyes darted from the lifeless form to his plow, then to the ever-deepening blanket of snow that could so easily conceal a multitude of sins.

"Damn it, Tim, think," he muttered to himself. His mind raced through scenarios, each more complex and dangerous than the last. But then, his eyes caught the bed of the plow truck—filled with a mixture of sand and salt, designed to give traction to vehicles on this icy night.

It was as if fate had laid out an option for him. Terrible, yet tantalizingly simple. With a grim resolve, Tim made his choice. He bent down, his back screaming in protest, and hoisted the man into his arms. Each step towards the truck felt like a descent, not just through the layers of snow, but through the strata of his own morality.

He laid the man in the truck's bed, atop the sand and salt. The ashen face looked almost peaceful now, a chilling serenity that only deepened Tim's inner turmoil. Shaking slightly, he pulled the tarp over the body, securing it against the biting wind and prying eyes.

As he climbed back into the cab, the weight of his choice settled over him, heavier than any snowfall. But there was no turning back now. Tim took a deep breath and screamed as he gripped the steering wheel, the snowflakes dancing in his headlights, like angels or demons.

He was not quite sure which.

As Tim's hand reached for the gearshift, a sudden burst of red and blue lights splashed across his rearview mirror. His heart, already laboring under the weight of his decision, skipped a beat. The police. Here, now, in the midst of this howling storm and his own spiraling panic.

Tim's eyes darted to the tarp-covered mound in the truck's bed. Had someone seen? Had he left some damning clue? His thoughts churned like the swirling snow around him, each flake a fragment of doubt, each gust of wind a breath of impending doom.

The officer's car door opened, a silhouette emerging against the glare of the headlights. The figure approached, but the storm was a curtain, veiling the man's identity. Tim's palms were clammy against the steering wheel, his breaths shallow and rapid. The footsteps crunched nearer, each step echoing in the cavern of Tim's anxiety.

Finally, the figure arrived at the window, and Tim rolled it down. A gust of snow-laden wind burst into the cab, but it was the face that froze him. Patrick. His ex-brother-in-law, and a Raven's Bend police officer. The eyes that had once looked at him across family dinners now evaluated him with professional scrutiny.

"Tim," Patrick said, his voice edged with a mix of surprise and suspicion, "how's the night treating you?"

Tim's throat tightened. The cab seemed to close in around him, walls inching nearer, air growing thin. Every instinct screamed to flee, but here he was, caught in the storm, in his choices, and now, in the steady gaze of Patrick.

Patrick repeated his question again. The words seemed to hang in the frigid air, crystallizing in the tension between them, but his eyes said more, probing for a crack in the façade.

"Ah, Patrick, it's, uh... it's going," Tim stammered, his voice betraying the nerves he fought to contain. "You know, another night, another storm."

"Mind stepping out of the cab for a moment?" Patrick's tone was level, but it was a command, not a request.

As Tim unbuckled his seatbelt, a surge of dread coursed through him. This was it. This was the moment when things could unravel. He opened the door and stepped out, feeling the cold seep through his layers and touch his skin like an omen.

It was then Patrick's eyes landed on the flask in the center console. The glint of metal stood out like a beacon in the dim light, damning evidence in a sea of otherwise mundane objects.

"Been drinking, Tim?" Patrick's words were ice-cold, devoid of any familial warmth they might have once held.

And there it was. The past, the present, and the dire future, converging at this very moment. Tim felt his world teetering on a precipice, as fragile as the snowflakes dissolving in the frigid air.

Tim's eyes darted nervously to the snow-covered ground behind him. The pristine layer of white had mercifully obscured any trace of the grim scene that had played out just minutes before. As if the heavens themselves had conspired to shroud his dark secret, at least for now.

Patrick motioned for Tim to follow a penlight with his eyes. Tim's gaze locked onto the small beam of light, his focus absolute, his movements deliberate. It was a dance of tension; the light swaying back and forth, Tim's eyes following it like a moth to a flame.

Finally, Patrick clicked off the penlight.

"Well, you're not drunk. But Tim, you've got to quit this," he gestured toward the cab. "I'll let you go tonight, but be careful. One of these nights, you won't be so lucky."

Relief washed over Tim like a warm wave breaking over a frigid shore.

"Yeah, Patrick, you're right. I will. Thank you," he said, his words laced with an emotion that was a mix of relief, gratitude, and a guilt that clawed at the walls of his conscience.

Patrick nodded, then walked back to his patrol car, the crunch of his boots in the snow growing fainter. Tim stood there, alone in the pooling darkness, the red and blue lights receding into the distance. The storm raged around him, but it was the tempest within that held him captive, frozen in place, as he contemplated the events of the night.

As the red and blue lights dissolved into the whiteness of the storm, Tim felt an itch of curiosity, a nagging concern mingled with self-preservation. Where had this man, dressed so incongruously for the weather, come from? The idea the man might have stumbled from a nearby house gnawed at Tim, a potential unraveling thread in the fabric of his perilous secret.

Switching on his flashlight, its beam cut through the darkness like a sword through a veil. After scanning his immediate surroundings, he noticed something. A path in the snow, barely visible under the accumulating flakes. It led away from the road, meandering into the skeletal trees that marked the entrance to the woods.

A chill deeper than the cold ran down Tim's spine. What was he doing? Should he just leave well enough alone? But something pulled him, a compulsion stronger than reason. His boots crunched on the fresh snow as he ventured into the woods, each step a commitment, each crunch a countdown to an unknown revelation.

The path twisted and turned, a labyrinth in the heart of the storm. Finally, the flashlight beam fell upon something. The edge of a clearing, and in it, the dark outline of old, dilapidated tombstones. A scattering of gravestones, some weathered and old, others newer but no less haunting. The beam of his flashlight danced over the etched names and dates, each a quiet testament to lives long gone.

Tim stood at the threshold of the cemetery, the wind carrying whispers of stories untold, as he pondered the grim irony of his find. He had sought answers, a clue to the identity of the man he'd struck. Instead, he found himself surrounded by the eternally silent, their secrets locked away beneath layers of earth and snow.

The beam of Tim's flashlight moved with a shaky hand, finally landing on a patch of disturbed earth. Fresh dirt lay strewn about, a chaotic pattern telling a chilling story. It was clear something—or someone—had dug their way out of the grave, not into it. The soil looked like it had erupted, a violent birth from the depths of the earth.

An icy shiver cascaded down Tim's spine, a dawning horror settling into the pit of his stomach. His light hesitated for a moment before climbing up to the face of the gravestone. The etched letters seemed to glow menacingly as the flashlight revealed the date of death: 1991. Over thirty years ago.

Time stood still. The wind, the snow, the crunching of his boots, all faded into a void of utter silence. He was alone in a clearing in the dead of night, confronting a horror that defied all reason and reality. The storm outside was a mere drizzle compared to the tempest now raging within him.

With his heart pounding in his chest, Tim retraced his steps, rushing back to the road. His eyes darted immediately to the back of his truck. A surge of panic jolted through him—the body was gone.

In a haze, Tim's gaze followed a fresh trail in the snow, a new set of footprints leading away from the truck. The trail veered toward River Road, a well-traveled route frequented by locals and outsiders alike, a stretch of asphalt that had borne witness to the comings and goings of Raven's Bend for years.

The familiar, often comforting sight of that road now twisted into something unrecognizable, tinged with an ominous undertone. Each falling snowflake seemed to mock him, contributing to a canvas that was painting his night in shades of unbelievable and horrifying.

Climbing into the cab of his truck, Tim reached for his flask with trembling hands. He took a long, slow sip, feeling the liquid burn its way down his throat and spread a fleeting warmth through his body. It was a futile attempt to drown the unimaginable, to wash away the contours of a night that had spiraled far beyond his grasp.

He revved the engine, the rumble of the plow a bass note in the eerie symphony of the storm. Gripping the steering wheel, he took one last glance at the fresh trail of footprints in his rearview mirror before pulling away. Each rotation of the wheels seemed a step further from the chilling reality he had stumbled into and an inch closer to the realm of disbelief.

As he drove on, past the snow-covered houses of Raven's Bend and down his well-remembered route, Tim wrestled with his own thoughts. A part of him yearned to deny the incomprehensible events of the night, to bury them deep within and plaster over them with the mundane routine of daily life.

Inside the fortified walls of his truck, Tim hurtled through the snowy night, the plow parting the white drifts like a ship through a stormy sea. The past hours had left him afloat in an ocean of unfathomable questions, and as he navigated through the familiar streets of his town, he couldn't help but wish for the blissful shores of ignorance, where this night would remain nothing more than a feverish dream, lost and forgotten in the coming dawn.

THIRD SHIFT WOES

Carson Arbogast stumbled and fought against the wind as he trudged through knee high snow back to the gate shack, his hand gripped vice-like on the assorted papers threatening to fly into the snowy darkness. The door flew open as soon as his gloved hand pulled down on the handle. Once inside, he pushed the door closed against the forceful wind. Even closed, the gusts whistled through the seam as snow and ice pelted against the large glass window. The semi pulled away, heading out into the storm, its empty trailer swaying in the gusts of wind.

The truck gate's bright florescent light cast a harsh white blanket over the interior, a stark contrast to the muted grays and whites swirling outside. As Carson sheltered within the truck gate's guard shack, the bright yellow lights of an approaching truck pierced through the blizzard's veil. He recognized the massive vehicle. A frequent delivery from a local potato farm. With practiced ease, he signaled the truck forward, and the driver guided the truck into the inbound lane with practiced ease.

Once parked, the driver, a broad-shouldered man named Dale, hopped out, snowflakes immediately clinging to his thick beard. He burst into the gate shack with less than his usual jovial exuberance. He greeted Carson with a grin that seemed slightly forced tonight.

"Rough one, eh?" Carson remarked, motioning towards the storm.

Dale grunted, rubbing at a spot on his hand concealed by a blood-soaked glove. "Storm's not the only rough part of this run," he muttered, his face shadowed with concern.

"You're bleeding? What happened?" Carson raised an eyebrow.

Dale hesitated for a second, then pulled up his sleeve, revealing a nasty-looking bite mark on his forearm.

"Picked up a hitchhiker on the river road back there. He was stumbling in the cold and seemed as if he was about to drop. He was wearing a black suit and tie, but he looked like he was death warmed over. The cold wasn't doing him any favors," he began. "Thought I'd help him out, y'know? But the guy… he went nuts. Bit me as soon as I opened the door to let him in. I kicked the asshole back out. He can freeze to death for all I care."

"You should get that checked, Dale." Carson stared, concern clear on his face.

"It's just a scratch. Probably just some druggie," he mumbled, waving his hand as he adjusted his sleeve back into place. "Anyway, better get this load processed."

Carson nodded, though the unease remained. "Stay safe out there. And seriously, you need a first aid kit for that?"

Dale simply gave a thumbs up and shook his head.

"I got one in the truck. I'll get it taken care of after I'm at the dock," he said, making his way towards the door.

As Carson glanced out of the window, a silhouette slowly materialized from the snowy curtain. As he neared the door, the shape solidified into Ben Chamerlain. Ben entered with his breath visible in the frigid air, exchanging a curt nod with Carson.

"Wild one tonight, huh?" Ben shouted over the howling wind, pulling his beanie down tighter. He pushed the door closed, stifling the roar slightly.

Carson chuckled, patting his replacement on the back. "Wouldn't be Maine if it wasn't trying to freeze us solid. Keep an eye on the Prime driver up at the top of the hill; he's been acting up tonight. I told him he couldn't park there and had to leave until his delivery time, but he hasn't listened. Good luck."

"I get all the fun drivers, don't I?" Ben chuckled as he logged into the PC and adjusted everything to his preferences.

As their brief chat concluded, Carson began his trek back to the main building. The swirling snowflakes seemed almost hypnotic, yet as he walked, a fleeting movement to his right caught his attention. A shadow darted between the shipping containers, just beyond the reach of the pale yard lights.

He paused, squinting into the darkness. The shadow was strangely elongated, and its movements seemed off, almost... predatory. Just as he was about to investigate further, the crackling sound of his radio broke the silence.

"Carson? It's Nancy," her voice sounded tense over the static. "That exit door by the west wing is pinging again. I think Ben might've left it ajar when he did his rounds. Can you check it out? The CCTV went out across the board, so I don't have any visibility anywhere."

Taken aback by the urgency in Nancy's voice, Carson hesitated for a moment, glancing once more at the spot where he'd seen the shadow. But with the snow and wind, everything seemed to blur together.

"Copy that," he replied, adjusting his course. "By the way, Nancy, we may have an animal in the yard. Can you put it on the log so we can check it out when the sun's up?"

"Sure thing," her voice crackled over his radio.

Carson pushed open the side entrance, the metallic scent of cold air mingling with the unique aroma of a vast industrial space. Immediately, the scale of the distribution center was both comforting and intimidating. Overhead, fluorescent lights illuminated rows upon rows of towering metal racks, each loaded with goods in various stages of packaging. The sheer scale of the place could be overwhelming, especially at night when only sections of the lights remained on, casting a patchwork of light and shadow over the facility.

Carson's boots made soft thuds against the polished concrete as he walked. The dim ambient light from the operational sections gave the dry side a ghostly hue. Every once in a while, a packaged item would catch the light oddly, its reflection briefly snagging his attention.

The quietude of the dry section was almost deafening after the howl of the storm outside. Carson was reminded why he always felt a bit uneasy patrolling this section at night. Without the regular hustle and bustle of daytime operations, the place felt abandoned, like the skeletal remains of its usual self.

As he ventured further, the distant hums grew louder, and the chilly atmosphere began to bite a bit more. The soft, ambient glow transitioned to the brighter, focused lights of the refrigerated sections. The change was almost palpable. Here, life persisted, even in the dead of night.

A few workers, bundled up in heavy gear, operated forklifts and moved about with purpose. Their breath visible in the cold air, they acknowledged Carson with quick nods or brief waves. The environment was colder, and the atmosphere thicker with the mist and moisture that clung to the refrigerated sections. There was comfort in seeing the workers. Signs of activity and normalcy in the vast, sometimes ominous setting of the distribution center.

Carson gave a nod to Jenna, a long-time third shift citizen, as she expertly maneuvered her forklift between aisles.

"Night, Carson," she called out, her voice slightly muffled by her thick scarf.

"Evening, Jenna," he replied, continuing towards the problematic door.

It wasn't long before he reached it, but as he approached, an uneasy feeling settled in. The door was not just ajar; it was wide open, and the gusts of wind carried flurries inside, making the ground near the doorway slick with a thin layer of ice.

He reached for his radio as he arrived at the door. Pulling it closed, he shook his head.

"Ben," he said after depressing the button to talk, "you left exit door A8 wide open, man. If it wouldn't take you a half hour to get back over here, I'd make you come and clean up this mess."

"Quit your whining," Ben replied, "and you're not the boss. David already went home for the night, and I know you're not going to call him for something like this." His laughter flooded the air before disconnecting.

"Boys, be nice," Nancy's jovial tones broadcasted over the comms, "Ben, I think you owe us. Carson for cleaning up your mess, and me, because I've had to listen to the alarm for the past twenty minutes."

Carson grabbed the bucket and mop, set next to this and every exit door for situations just like this. He grumbled as he wrung out the mop into a yellow bucket. The water had already started to form a thin icy layer near the door, a clear hazard for any of the workers. He made a mental note to check back in with this location before day shift started in a few hours.

As he moved the mop back and forth, he noticed something peculiar. Amidst the wet smears, there was a clear imprint of a shoe. And then another. But as he followed the progression of these footprints, Carson noted an odd pattern: a solid left footprint, then a messy, smeared mark, almost like... a drag.

A drag leading into the warehouse. As if someone entered from outside.

He stood upright; the mop handle resting against his shoulder, and traced the footprints with his gaze. They continued into the warehouse, the pattern consistent, a step, then a drag. The right foot appeared as if it had never fully planted, leaving behind a streaked trail.

The unease that had settled in Carson's stomach earlier returned in full force. The storm outside, the rumbling of the metal framed warehouse, Dale's strange encounter, and now these footprints, left a pit in his stomach.

Cautiously, Carson set the mop aside and reached for his flashlight, switching it on. The focused beam pierced the dimness, revealing more of the dragging footprints as they snaked deeper into the vast expanse of the distribution center down the cereal aisle.

He clicked his radio, "Nancy, I've got something here. Some... footprints. Doesn't look right. I'm going to follow them, see where they lead. Unless Ben is screwing with me?"

"Not me," Ben's voice crackled from the speaker.

The static of the radio crackled for a moment before Nancy's voice responded, "Be careful, Carson. Do you want me to send over the dock manager from the cold desk?"

Carson shook his head, then chuckled to himself.

"I'm good," he responded. "I'll radio if I see anything. It's honestly probably some driver who got lost in the snow trying to find the Receiving Office."

The trail of footprints led Carson toward the cereal aisle. This section was a long row of towering shelves, each laden with oversized cardboard boxes containing the vibrantly colored boxes of cereal found in the stores. As Carson's flashlight beam swept across the floor, catching glimpses of the footprints, a soft rustling sound caught his attention. He halted, shining the light further up the aisle. At first, nothing seemed out of place, just rows of cereals lined up neatly. But then, in the deeper shadows of an intersecting corridor, he noticed something.

A figure, standing still, seemingly watching him.

The man stood there, dressed in a pristine black suit, complete with a sharp tie. The dim lighting obscured most of his features, but the suit was unmistakable. Carson almost laughed at the absurdity.

"Hello?" Carson called out, his voice echoing slightly. "Are you okay? It's dangerous to be outside, especially during a storm. Were you just out walking on River Road?"

The man didn't respond, his form unmoving, just continuing to stare from the shadows. Carson heard the man's ragged breaths echoing in the empty warehouse. Carson took a step forward, his flashlight firmly trained on the figure.

"Sir, you can't be here. I'm with Asset Protection. I need to escort you out."

It was then that the man shifted. But it wasn't a natural movement. His head tilted to an odd angle, and Carson caught a glimpse of the man's eyes, glazed over and devoid of life. The distinct drag mark Carson had been following now made a chilling sense.

Bile rose in Carson's throat, and a primal piece of his brain buzzed. His breathing slowed as watched the man.

The suited figure took a shuffling step forward, the dragging foot echoing softly in the quietness. Carson slowly retreated, but he broke into a sprint, his flashlight's beam dancing erratically as adrenaline coursed through him.

The eerie stillness shattered as the suited man suddenly lunged, moving with an unsettling, jerky speed. Carson stumbled back in surprise, his heart pounding. The flashlight beam caught the full view of the man as he emerged from the shadows. His skin stretched, ashen gray across his face, as he looked on with eyes clouded and vacant, and his lips parted revealing teeth stained with a dark, viscous liquid.

Carson sprinted faster, weaving between the tall shelves. The sounds of the man's relentless pursuit echoed behind him, the unmistakable shuffle and drag of its gait interspersed with raspy growls. He dared a glance back and saw the creature reaching out with clawed hands, its mouth snapping hungrily. Carson made a sharp turn into another aisle, knocking over a stack of boxes hoping to slow it down.

Without warning, the zombie lunged at him from around the corner, catching the edge of Carson's coat. Carson could feel the pressure as the creature bit down hard. Panic surged as he awaited the sharp pain of teeth breaking skin, but to his surprise and relief, the thick material of his coat held firm, preventing the teeth from penetrating.

The pressure from the creature's bite relented as Carson shoved it away. Using his flashlight, he struck at it over and over, but it made no difference to the creature. Carson quickly scanned his surroundings. Above him, the towering racks held a variety of cargo, including empty pallets. He saw them used for a myriad of purposes during the day, from transport to makeshift repairs and anything in between. He pulled himself to his feet and rushed toward a blue wood pallet sitting on the rollers at chest height.

The creature, recovering from the glare of the flashlight, lunged again. This time, Carson was prepared. With a calculated sidestep, he dodged the creature and positioned himself beside the empty pallet. He then tugged at the wood, popping it off of the end stop.

For a tense moment, nothing happened.

Then, with a groan of stressed and splintering wood, the pallet shifted with the full pallet of freight behind it pushing. The creature, sensing the impending danger but unable to process it, looked up just in time for the empty pallet to slam into its face.

There was a sickening crunch, and the suited man was instantly silenced, his head crushed beneath the weight. The rest of his body spasmed momentarily before becoming still. Carson stood there, chest heaving, taking in the aftermath as something black oozed from the head of the man at his feet. He stepped back and leaned against the metal racking.

Carson, still trembling from the adrenaline rush, snatched his radio as Nancy's voice crackled through. "Carson, Steve, and Maggie over in Receiving just called about Dale. They said he's making some weird noises in the bathroom. Are you near there? Can you go check it out?"

Before Carson could even process the request, let alone inform Nancy about the horror he had just faced, a piercing scream echoed through the otherwise quiet warehouse, emanating from the direction of the receiving dock. The scream was cut short, replaced by an unsettling silence that seemed to spread through the sprawling structure. His heart sinking, Carson broke into a run.

"Nancy, there's something really wrong happening here," he gasped into the radio, his voice trembling. "I need to go check on them. Get everyone to the cafeteria and lock the doors, now!"

Without waiting for a response, Carson continued sprinting towards the receiving area, his breaths short and panicked. His mind raced with the unfolding nightmare, each scream painting a vivid picture of the terror spreading through the warehouse. As he approached the receiving area, he could hear more distressed noises, the sounds of struggle, of desperation. He knew he was running towards danger but continued forward.

The scene that greeted him as he burst into the receiving dock was one of chaos and bloodshed. Dale, now a grotesque version of his former self, was in the midst of attacking Steve while Maggie twitched nearby, bloody and broken. Carson skidded to a stop. Dale gave him no notice as he continued to claw and bite Steve with chunks of meat scattered on his beard. Dale paused and lifted his head as Maggie stirred.

Carson's eyes then darted to Maggie, who lay twitching on the floor, a pool of dark blood around her. Carson's heart sank, but before he could process the tragic scene, something extraordinary and horrifying occurred. Maggie's body twitched, then shuddered violently before her head snapped up, her eyes now a dull, lifeless gray. Carson watched in horror as Maggie, now a grotesque version of herself, unsteadily rose to her feet. The woman he knew, cheerful and kind, was replaced by this. This monster moving with a chilling, predatory grace.

Meanwhile, Dale had finished with Steve, whose lifeless body now lay on the floor. But much like Maggie, after a haunting moment of stillness, Steve's body twitched and convulsed as he, too, joined the ranks of the undead. Carson's breath caught in his throat. He struggled to breathe. He stood frozen at the grim display before him.

Carson's blood ran cold as Nancy's voice crackled through the radio, breaking the silence. "Carson, what's going on over there? Respond!"

The abrupt noise drew the attention of the monstrosities in the room. All three heads, Maggie, Steve, and Dale, snapped towards him, their eyes vacant yet fixated on him with a bone-chilling intensity. In that horrific moment, the grotesque trio lunged towards Carson, the expressions of hunger on their twisted faces sending terror coursing through his veins.

Carson's survival instincts kicked in with a ferocious urgency. He spun on his heels and sprinted down the aisle, his breaths fast and shallow, each one echoing sharply through the quiet warehouse. The sounds of the pursuing undead were a monstrous cacophony chasing him through the dark, lifeless corridors.

His mind raced as he darted through the maze-like setup of the warehouse, desperately trying to put distance between himself and the pursuing horrors. The urgency in Nancy's voice on the radio seemed a world away as he focused solely on escaping the immediate danger.

The screams of the creatures echoed through the steel and concrete canyons of the warehouse as Carson darted blindly through the towers of metal racks and pallets of dry goods.

Carson's frantic sprint carried him across one of the large forklift doors separating the dry section from the refrigerated area of the warehouse. As he barged through the barrier of air between the two, a cloud of frosty air engulfed him, the cold instantly biting into his skin. He skidded to a halt, glancing back to gauge the position of his pursuers.

To his astonishment, the trio hesitated at the threshold of the cold zone. They milled about uncertainly, their rage and anger seemingly at odds with the freezing temperatures that lay beyond the door. His mind raced as he backed further into the cold section, keeping his eyes on the monsters who continued to linger at the door, growling and snapping, but not daring to cross into the chilled area.

His radio crackled again with Nancy's voice, her words a mixture of concern and urgency, "Carson! Are you there? What's happening?"

"I don't know, Nancy, but call the police. Get everyone out of here. Get everyone outside."

Nancy's voice crackled through the radio, her tone a blend of disbelief and concern. "Carson, are you out of your mind? It's a whiteout blizzard out there! And what do you mean, call 911? What the hell is going on?"

Carson's breaths came fast as he tried to find the words, the horror of what he had witnessed still threatening to choke him. "Nancy, you won't believe me until you see it yourself, but the warehouse... it's turned into a nightmare. I was... attacked by... I don't know, they seemed like... zombies. Dale, Maggie, Steve... they're... they're not human anymore. Just... just trust me and get everyone outside. We need help. We need it now!"

The following silence felt like an eternity as Carson awaited Nancy's response, the cold seeping through his bones, yet providing a strange semblance of safety for the moment.

Finally, Nancy's voice came through, filled with a blend of urgency and concern, "Carson, not everyone is out. I can't get a response from the freezer crew. They were adamant about finishing their routes... Tell me what's going on."

Carson felt a knot tighten in his stomach. He clenched the radio tighter and tighter until his hand shook with slight tremors.

"Dammit," he muttered under his breath, grappling with the harsh reality of the situation. "Nancy, keep trying to reach them. I'll... I'll try to get to them. There's no time to explain. And make that call to 911. We need every help we can get."

As if summoned by the grim discussion, the large door to the freezer section rolled up as the chains spun, spilling a group of about ten employees into the refrigerated area. They were talking in loud, hurried tones, oblivious to the terror awaiting in the dry section. The first two forklifts pushed through before Carson managed to shout a warning.

The gruesome trio waiting lunged from the shadows, their grotesque forms a blur as they descended upon the unsuspecting crew. Tamsin Sinclair, with her freezer bibs hanging around her waist, and Harlan Cobb, already wearing just a T-shirt as he sped toward the breakroom, were yanked off their forklifts with vicious force, their screams echoing through the cold air as the monsters sunk their teeth into flesh.

"Over here!" Carson yelled, beckoning frantically to the remaining workers who had evaded the initial assault. They sprinted towards him, their faces pale and eyes wide with horror. The grim reality of the nightmare they had found themselves in was beginning to sink in with every blood-curdling scream that echoed through the warehouse. As Carson caught his breath, the chilling screams of his colleagues mingled with the howling wind of the blizzard outside.

With a heavy breath, Carson looked over to Lila Tremblay, the shipping manager known for her steely resolve. She nodded, and together they marshaled the frightened employees into a semblance of order. Each breath hung in the chilly air as they prepared to move through the nightmarish landscape of the once-familiar warehouse. The flickering overhead lights cast long, ghostly shadows as the group cautiously moved through the aisles, their every step a crunch on the debris scattered across the floor. Every clatter echoed through the eerie silence, sending shivers down their spines. On the other side of the metal wall, the group of their former coworkers and friends scratched along as Carson and his charges moved through the refrigerated rooms.

At the next air gate, the creatures, now five monstrous forms, pushed into the blowing air between the dry section and the refrigerated section. They tested the cold further and further as they clawed and reached for the survivors. They approached the cafeteria, a place once filled with laughter and conversation, now a hopeful sanctuary amidst the horror. Carson could feel the tension among the group as a palpable force, every small sound making them twitch, eyes darting into the dark corners.

"Nancy," Carson radioed, "Nancy, is everyone in the breakroom?" Carson tried to peer around the creatures in the door, but found himself unable to see the cafeteria across the way.

"Carson," Nancy's voice bleated from his radio, a mix between a cry and a scream, "something happened in the cafeteria. A driver wandered in and started attacking us. It was chaos in there! Then everyone started attacking. When it started, I ran to the office and locked it down, and now they're hammering at the security office door. I'm locked in, but I don't know how long it'll hold! The police said they are on their way, but with the storm, who knows when they'll be here?"

Carson's group went silent, every face turning to Carson. Lila Tremblay's eyes met his, both filled with the same unspoken question: What now?

With the reality of their predicament sinking in, the room's atmosphere grew thick with tension. Carson and Lila exchanged a long, contemplative look. It was a silent dialogue carrying the weight of desperate options and the precarious balance between life and death. A hushed conversation started among the survivors, each contributing fragments of ideas hovering in the cold air like delicate shards of glass.

Amid the low rumble of whispered deliberations, a voice arose from the corner of the room. Mary, one of the maintenance workers who usually kept to herself, her eyes perpetually shielded by the brim of her cap, lifted her hand.

"Listen," she said, "we've got the weight of the storm's ice on the roof right above this section, right? And there hasn't been time to clear off the ice from the last one. What if we used the forklifts to knock out the support beams? Draw these monsters into the refrigerated area and let the roof come down on them?"

The room went quiet, all eyes turning toward Mary. Carson weighed her words. His mouth moved slightly as he contemplated the plan. Lila looked at Carson, her eyes narrowing as she mentally calculated the logistics, the potential to actually pull this off.

"It's a huge risk," she said, "but if we're precise and quick, we could localize the collapse. And with the blizzard, the ice and snow would essentially entomb whatever's underneath. It might work."

"Alright," he spoke, his voice steady despite the churning uncertainty within. "It's a plan, but how do we get them in here?" He looked to the air gate. "All of them."

"The climate controls in the main office. Can Nancy adjust things? Can she cool it down out there? Warm it up in here?"

"I think so." Carson nods thoughtfully.

A slab of ground beef wrapped in clear plastic dropped in front of Carson. He looked up to see Mary standing there with an arm full of refrigerated meat packages.

"Think we can make is tempting to come in here?"

"Can't hurt," Lila smiled. She stood and looked around at her crew and shouted, "Alright folks, let's prep the forklifts. We've got a roof to bring down."

"Nancy," Carson radioed Nancy, "Nancy, no time to explain, but I need you to start adjusting the climate controls for the building. I want you to start cooling down the offices and open the dampers on the dry side. Let the cold in.

As they sprang into action, Mary explaining to them which beams would need to be struck and with which piece of equipment, Carson could not help but feel a mixture of dread and determination. They were adrift in a sea of horror, and this plan, reckless as it might be, was the last glimmer of a lighthouse on a stormy night.

The forklifts roared to life with a mechanical growl that echoed the collective anxiety of the room. Carson and Lila coordinated the operation, their voices bouncing across the room, as the rest of the team positioned themselves near the emergency exit, ready to bolt at Carson's signal. The refrigerated section hummed with tension, each individual keenly aware that the line between salvation and catastrophe was perilously thin.

As the forklifts charged toward the designated support beams, the noise attracted the attention of the monstrous figures beyond the air gate. Like moths to a flame, they shuffled into the refrigerated section, their guttural sounds a cacophony of impending doom. It was a grim parade lured by the spectacle of their own destruction, though they had no way of knowing it.

The first beam cracked under the force of the forklifts, a disconcerting sound that ricocheted through the room. Then the second, the third. Each creak and groan of the structure seemed to question the sanity of their actions. Just as doubt flooded Carson's mind, he felt the unmistakable shift in the air, a sudden drop in pressure that heralded imminent collapse.

"NOW!" he yelled to the others, his voice tinged with a blend of urgency and finality. Every pair of eyes met his, and then, as one, they turned and sprinted for the emergency exit. Lila was the last to leave, casting a final glance over her shoulder as the ceiling gave way.

They burst through the emergency door into the freezing embrace of the blizzard outside, as behind them, the roof surrendered to the weight of the storm. With a deafening roar, it came crashing down, obliterating everything in its path, including the nightmarish figures that had invaded their sanctuary.

As they stood there, panting and shivering in the cold, the reality of their narrow escape settled in. The warehouse, their place of employment, was now a tomb encased in ice and darkness. The blizzard raged on around them, indifferent to the horror it had concealed.

Amidst the relentless howl of the blizzard, a wail of sirens sliced through the air, a discordant symphony signaling both rescue and the end of anonymity for what had transpired. Police cars and ambulances skidded down the icy entrance ramp, emergency lights spinning their red and blue auras into the snowy darkness. The ethereal glow danced across the faces of the survivors, turning each into a portrait of relief and trauma.

Carson stood apart. His eyes met Lila's for a brief moment before he turned back to the approaching vehicles. The pulsating colors washed over his visage, casting him in alternating shades of urgency and melancholy. It was as though each flash of light sought to penetrate the emotional armor he had donned, revealing glimpses of a man forever changed by the night's horrors.

As the first responders disembarked, their faces set in grim determination, their actions methodical despite the chaos, Carson felt a strange detachment settling over him. It was as if he were caught in the eye of another storm, this one far more introspective, composed of questions with answers he was not yet prepared to face.

In that fleeting interlude, caught between the world he once knew and an uncertain future, he felt the weight of stories yet untold, judgments yet rendered, and truths yet revealed. And then, as if letting go of a breath he had been holding all along, Carson felt himself surrender to the moment, to the arrival of accountability and the reckoning it would inevitably bring.

As emergency responders buzzed around the scene, orchestrating the chaos into some semblance of order, a police officer approached Carson, notebook in hand.

"Sir, can you tell me what happened here? We need to get an initial statement for the record."

Carson locked eyes with Lila and Mary, who stood a few feet away amidst the crowd of survivors. For a heartbeat, their glances exchanged a world of unspoken understanding, a secret compact forged in the crucible of their harrowing ordeal.

"The roof collapsed," Carson said, his voice imbued with a finality that brooked no further inquiry.

The officer nodded, scribbled something into his notebook, and moved on to the next individual, unaware of the gravity that lingered in the three words just spoken.

And so, in the cold Maine night, surrounded by the ephemeral blaze of red and blue lights, each person stood as if suspended in a moment outside of time. Then, almost inaudibly, as if whispered by the wind, the chapter closed. There would be more questions, more stories, more nights forever imprinted in their memories, but not tonight. Tonight, they stood together in the silent aftermath, each encased in their own narrative, bound by a truth that would remain unspoken but never forgotten.

.

The Overpass

The blizzard engulfing Raven's Bend had finally dissipated, its white-out fury relenting to a brittle, predawn calm. The sky, gradually shedding its shroud of storm clouds, hinted at the first light of day, and as streetlights flickered over the snow-coated roads, their glow barely penetrated the icy mist still clinging to the air.

Detective Charlie Langlois drove his cruiser cautiously through the still-quiet streets, tires crunching over packed snow. His police radio broke the silence, carrying reports that felt both routine and increasingly alarming.

"David Allen's family reported him missing last night. We can't officially do anything yet, but if a unit's near Hillcrest Drive, they might want to swing by and check on the family," the dispatcher noted. The news was disquieting; David Allen was well known around town, and a disappearance during a blizzard posed risks that didn't need spelling out.

"Additionally, heard there was a roof collapse at the distribution center over on Mill Road. EMS is on site, still getting details," the dispatcher continued. The weight of the storm was both literal and figurative, it seemed.

Charlie sighed, the weight of Raven's Bend's unfolding dramas pressing against him. This town, a repository of both dreams and nightmares, held a unique gravitational pull on its residents. He switched off the radio as he approached Durham Road, where the interstate overpass loomed like an obsidian monolith against the graying sky.

Parking his cruiser, he stepped out onto the icy pavement. Pulling his coat tightly around him, he moved closer to the scene that awaited him. Police tape had already been strung up, its yellow contrasting starkly against the snow, marking the area where something unspeakable had occurred.

Inhaling deeply, Charlie braced himself for another descent into the complicated, often dark, intricacies of life in Raven's Bend. Here, in the shadow of the overpass, he would once again search for fragments of truth in a world that seemed increasingly unwilling to give them up.

Charlie's boots crunched over the snow as he crossed the police tape, his breath visible in the frigid air. The scene before him was jarring, even to his veteran eyes. The overpass, usually a simple construct of concrete and steel, had been transformed into a macabre stage.

Beneath the shadow of the interstate, an array of symbols had been etched into the ground, partially obscured by snow but discernible to the trained eye. At the center lay the victim, positioned with a gruesome deliberateness that hinted at ritualistic intent. The body was adorned with odd talismans and offerings, each carefully placed as though part of some dark liturgy.

"Who could do something like this?" muttered Officer Henderson, who had been first on the scene and was visibly shaken.

"Someone who understands the theatrics of cruelty all too well," Charlie replied, his eyes not leaving the unsettling scene before him.

The detective snapped on a pair of latex gloves, crouching down to inspect the scene. Each detail, however minute, could be a breadcrumb leading to whoever had committed this abominable act. He felt the heaviness of the moment, the silent urgency that always accompanied the first hours of an investigation. There was a killer to catch, one who had turned the innocuous over-pass into an altar of horrors.

Finally, Charlie stood up, removing his gloves and disposing of them carefully. He took a deep breath, his gaze moving from the grisly scene to the town that spread out before over the Androscoggin River. Raven's Bend was a complicated tapestry, its threads weaving beauty and malevolence in intricate patterns that defied easy understanding.

"Get the evidence team here. And tell dispatch to update the chief. We're going to need all hands on deck for this one," Charlie ordered, his tone hardened by the gravity of what lay before him. As his team sprang into action, Charlie took one last look at the victim, a silent vow forming in his mind. Whoever had done this would not find sanctuary in Raven's Bend. Not on his watch.

In the half-light of dawn, Charlie Langlois moved through the grim presentation, his leather-soled shoes crunching on the frost-covered ground beneath the overpass. The wind whispered secrets, carrying a chill that cut through his coat, as if cautioning him of the shadows he was about to enter.

"Damn, sir, this looks like those killings back in the '40s," Officer Miller said, appearing beside him. His breath clouded instantly in the frigid air, adding to the atmosphere of unease.

"Old town tales, Miller. But this," Charlie's voice trailed off, his eyes scrutinizing the intricate symbols carved into the ground around the body. "This is methodical, planned. It's like the killer wanted us to find it."

The weather seemed to react; the wind gaining an unsettling momentum, swirling as if roused by their conversation. Charlie returned his attention to the scene before him, pondering how the elements themselves, the very fabric of Raven's Bend, seemed to reverberate with the dread he felt. Each clue he unearthed only deepened the enigma, knotting it further into the town's already dark history.

And throughout it all, the wind and cold watched, as if Raven's Bend itself waited to see how he would unravel this twisted web of death and obscurity.

Charlie squatted down next to the body, his gloved hands carefully picking up a tattered student ID card that lay a few feet away. Dried blood splattered across the plastic, but the name and photograph were mostly visible. "Jessie Loomis, Grove University," he read softly.

His eyes shifted to the victim, whose features had been rendered almost unrecognizable through the violence inflicted upon them. There was no way to confirm at this moment if the ID belonged to the body on the cold ground.

"Could be a red herring," Officer Miller suggested, peering over Charlie's shoulder at the ID. "But it could also be our way into understanding who did this."

"The killer either made a mistake or wants us to find this," Charlie mused, rising back to his full height. His gaze met Miller's, then both looked back at the grim scene. "Either way, it's a lead. And right now, that's all we've got."

The wind howled in response, as if in agreement, whipping itself into frenzied gusts that seemed to envelop the overpass. It felt as if even the air had taken a vested interest in their investigation, as each clue added another layer to the disturbing mosaic of events.

Charlie sighed as he picked up the student ID from the passenger seat, bagged in clear plastic as evidence. "Dispatch, this is Detective Langlois. I'm heading to Grove University to follow up on a lead related to the overpass case."

"Acknowledged, Detective. Keep us posted," came the reply through the radio.

He started the cruiser and cautiously navigated through the freshly plowed roads. As he drove along the river, he reflected on his destination. Grove University—its very name often meant dealing with naïve, inexperienced college kids who thought they knew it all. A mild annoyance crept in as he thought about the likely interactions ahead.

Driving into the downtown area, he noticed that life was slowly returning post-storm. Shops were opening, the flicker of their lights muted by the layers of snow still clinging to the windowpanes.

Soon enough, he arrived at Grove University. The elegant brick buildings wore a coat of snow, as if dressed for the season. He parked the cruiser and turned off the engine, contemplating the campus before him. It was a place he didn't particularly enjoy visiting, but duty called.

Charlie stepped out of the cruiser, pulling his coat tighter against the biting cold. The campus was mostly quiet, a dormant sprawl of stone and brick resting beneath its blanket of snow. Students were few and far between at this early hour, their eyes hidden behind puffy jackets and fur-lined hoods.

He held up the student ID to the few passersby he encountered. Most offered no more than shrugs or head shakes. Just when he thought he'd come up empty-handed, a young woman clutching a steaming cup of coffee squinted at the ID and said, "Yeah, I think he lives in Alden Hall, over there."

She pointed to a four-story building across the snow-covered quad. "Thanks," he mumbled, making his way towards the building with renewed purpose. Alden Hall: a name he remembered from previous, less grim investigations. The snow crunched under his boots as he covered the distance, his breath visible in the icy air. He couldn't shake the feeling that the winter, with its relentless chill, was watching him, as if it too were curious about the dark tale unfolding.

Charlie reached Alden Hall and spotted a young man fumbling with keys in front of one of the doors. The guy looked agitated, repeatedly glancing over his shoulder as he knocked on the door, louder each time.

"What's going on here?" Charlie inquired, approaching them.

The young man glanced up, surprised. "I'm Greg, a friend of Jessie. He didn't come back last night, and he's not answering his phone or texts. I was getting worried."

Just then, a young woman with a name badge reading "RA-Melissa" appeared from down the hallway, her eyes narrowed with a mix of curiosity and concern.

"Is there a problem?" she asked.

Charlie revealed his badge. "Detective Langlois, Raven's Bend PD. I need to get inside this room."

Melissa hesitated only for a moment before unlocking the door. The tension hung in the air, as thick as the morning fog that had settled on the river. Charlie stepped inside, his eyes scanning the room, knowing that each detail might be a clue in the grim puzzle he was assembling.

Inside, the room was dimly lit; the curtains drawn tight. But even in the subdued light, what caught Charlie's eye immediately was hard to miss. Occult paraphernalia filled the room, candles with arcane symbols etched into the wax, multiple books on the shelf with titles like "Necromancy Across the World" and "Rites of the Damned," and an intricate pentagram rug laid out on the floor.

The atmosphere was thick, suffused with a sense of impending doom that matched the lingering, overcast skies outside. It was like stepping into another world, one where the veil between the natural and supernatural seemed to blur.

"Would you look at this?" Charlie mumbled, his voice tinged with disbelief and a spike of dread. He reached for his radio. "Dispatch, this is Langlois. I'm at Grove University. You won't believe what I've found. We may have a lead on our case."

For a moment, he glanced back at Greg and Melissa, their faces registering shock and confusion. "You folks might want to step back," he advised. Charlie eyed the room's disquieting contents one more time before turning his attention back to Greg and Melissa. "Do either of you know where Jessie might be right now?"

Greg shifted uncomfortably before answering, "Well, he's been spending a lot of time at the old Lubric farm on Shale Road. Said he found something there that could 'change everything.'"

A wave of recognition washed over Charlie. Shale Road was just a few turns away from the overpass. "Thank you, both of you. Please don't leave campus until we've sorted all of this out."

Reaching for his radio, he called in, "Dispatch, Langlois here. I've got a lead that takes me near the crime scene. Send a patrol over to the college to bag and tag the room. I'm heading to Shale Road, the old Lubric place."

As he stepped out into the frigid morning air, his gaze met the brooding clouds that hung low. It was almost as if the storm itself was in on this grim tapestry, a silent witness to unfolding events.

Charlie slid back into his cruiser, starting the engine and letting it idle for a moment as he thought through the information he'd gathered. With a deep sigh, he pulled away from Grove University, his tires crunching on the freshly salted roads.

The town's storefronts faded into his rearview mirror, replaced by snow-cloaked fields and barren trees. The day's feeble light barely touched the expanse of whiteness, as if timid to disturb the aftermath of the storm. Soon, Raven's Bend was behind him, its stately Victorian homes and bustling businesses giving way to the rural outskirts.

He turned onto Shale Road, the cruiser's headlights cutting through the lingering morning mist. As he drove, the snow beneath his tires felt compacted, unyielding. The weight of what lay ahead tightened in his chest. What would he find at the old Lubric farm? The pieces were aligning in a pattern he wasn't sure he was ready to confront.

Nearing his destination, Charlie felt a cold rush of air seep through the car's vents, as if the storm was reminding him it still held sway over this quiet countryside. He gripped the steering wheel a bit tighter, eyes narrowing as the dilapidated barn of the Lubric farm came into view.

Stepping out of his cruiser, Charlie stood for a moment, surveying the rundown Lubric farm. The once-red paint of the barn had peeled away, revealing graying, splintered wood beneath. A rusty wind vane squeaked in the early morning breeze, its arrow aimlessly spinning atop the cupola. The rest of the farm was just as dilapidated, a collapsed chicken coop, barbed-wire fencing sagging under the weight of years, and an old farmhouse with shattered windows that stood like vacant eyes. A fresh blanket of snow covered everything. Everything except for the tracks leading to a car parked near the barn.

His eyes fell upon the vehicle, a sedan covered in a thin layer of frost, sporting a Grove University bumper sticker. A sense of urgency now replaced his earlier reluctance. Snow crunched beneath his boots as he moved closer, the purity of the white expanse making the scene feel all the more surreal. He reached for his radio, announcing his location to the officers on duty.

With one last glance at the horizon, where the grays of dawn surrendered to the brighter hues of day, Charlie reached for the car's door handle. Every detail, from the new snow to the ominous storm clouds retreating in the distance, coalesced into a moment of unsettling clarity. This quiet, abandoned farm was the setting for something much darker than he could have ever anticipated.

The crunch of snow under Charlie's boots seemed unnaturally loud in the still, post-storm air. He advanced cautiously, gun drawn and aimed low, his eyes locked on the slightly ajar barn door. A sliver of dim light leaked out, painting a thin line across the freshly fallen snow. The old barn itself looked as if it had suffered years of neglect, its wooden panels weathered and warped.

Stopping a few feet from the entrance, he took a steadying breath. His gloved hand hovered near the weathered wood of the door, hesitating. Years on the force had taught him that scenes like this often veered into the unpredictable. The barn's silence felt almost oppressive, weighing on him as he stood there, gun in hand, contemplating his next move.

Charlie nudged the barn door open with his boot, the creaking hinges cutting through the silence like a discordant note. As the door swung wider, the viscous scene inside revealed itself. His eyes locked onto Jessie, kneeling beside a flickering black candle. Beside him lay another body, displayed in a manner eerily reminiscent of the scene at the overpass.

His heart pounding, Charlie raised his weapon and aimed it squarely at Jessie. "Raven's Bend PD! Stand up slowly and step away from the body!"

Jessie looked up, his eyes hollow, almost resigned, as if he'd been expecting this moment. Yet, behind that resignation, Charlie thought he saw something darker, an ember of something he couldn't quite name.

The barn seemed to close in around them, the stale air thickening. It was a moment suspended in time, laden with a gravity that transcended the grisly scene, as if the walls themselves held their breath in anticipation.

Jessie's voice broke the silence, quivering under the weight of his sorrow. "I was promised, you know? Promised she'd come back to me."

Charlie kept his gun trained on him, but his eyes narrowed, taking in the layers of despair and desperation etched into Jessie's face.

"I was promised," Jessie repeated, as if saying the words enough times could rewrite the surrounding reality, could bring back the love he'd lost.

In that moment, the atmosphere inside the barn felt even heavier, as if charged with the weight of broken promises and shattered dreams. Each utterance of 'promised' reverberated through the space, mingling with the acrid scent of burnt candle wax and fresh snow wafting through the cracks in the wooden walls.

"Jessie, let me help you," Charlie urged, his voice tinged with a reluctant compassion he couldn't quite stifle.

"I was promised," Jessie continued, his focus unbreaking, as if stuck in a loop of his own despair.

"Who promised you, Jessie?" Charlie pressed, but the young man gave no response. He simply knelt there, a broken figure in a perverted feat of desperation, surrounded by the macabre evidence of his misguided attempts to regain what he'd lost. The silence that followed felt as oppressive as the weight of the fresh snow accumulating outside.

"Jessie, lay down and put your hands behind your head. It's over," Charlie commanded, his eyes focused and unwavering.

Instead, Jessie rose to his feet, turning to face Charlie. In his hand, he brandished a knife, the same chilling weapon that had likely brought an end to the life on the floor beside him. The atmosphere in the barn seemed to tighten, mirroring the tension that gripped the air between the two men.

"Jessie, think about what you're doing," Charlie urged, his voice tinged with a desperate calm. "You don't want to add another life to this madness. Put the knife down."

As he spoke, the black candle beside Jessie began to pulse. It emitted an unnatural light, its rhythm almost mirroring the beating of a heart. A sense of foreboding swept over Charlie; the room itself seemed to shudder in response to the candle's eerie glow.

A subtle pull in the recesses of his mind tugged at Charlie, like a fisherman's line cast into the depths of his consciousness. It felt as if whispered words were circling, just beyond comprehension.

"You can hear it too?" Jessie's eyes widened, and the knife in his hand lowered a fraction.

The whispers seemed to crescendo, building into a murmur that resonated within the walls of Charlie's skull. "What is going on?" he croaked out, fighting the mounting disorientation.

Jessie's eyes flickered between Charlie and the pulsating candle. "My girlfriend died a few weeks ago. I found this place, and this book," he gestured vaguely at a tattered tome lying on a wooden table near the flickering candle. "It promised me I could bring her back. All I had to do was offer another life to… to whatever is whispering."

His voice quivered, dissonance shadowing his features. "I tried it once already, with the first victim. I felt the ritual work, but it didn't give me what I wanted. She's not back. But it promised," he emphasized, almost desperately, "it promised she'd return. So, I had to try again."

The whispers converged, blending into a singular voice that seemed to emanate from the very air, as if the barn itself were speaking. The candle's pulsing grew more frantic, its light nearly blinding.

"You can hear it too, can't you?" Jessie looked at Charlie, his eyes searching for confirmation. "Promises, always promises."

Charlie tightened his grip on his gun, his knuckles turning white. The voice was clear now, like an intimate whisper in his ear, dangling promises before him, promises that plucked at the frayed edges of his own desires and fears. A chill ran down his spine, colder than the air outside, as he realized the seductive pull the voice must have had on Jessie.

Charlie shook his head, as if the physical motion could dislodge the intoxicating voice from his mind. "Jessie, we need to leave. Now. This isn't the way."

Jessie hesitated, his eyes shifting from the candle to Charlie, as if caught in a tug-of-war between two worlds. The air grew thick with tension, each second stretching out as they both battled the siren song of promises unfulfilled.

Jessie's gaze fell upon the pulsing candle one last time, murmuring, "I was promised," as if that absolution could make all the wrongs right. With a sudden burst of manic energy, he lunged at Charlie, knife brandished high.

Instinct and training took over. Charlie sidestepped the lunge just in time, aiming his gun and pulling the trigger. The bullet found its mark, embedding itself into Jessie's chest. Jessie's face registered shock and disbelief as he stumbled back, clutching the spreading red stain over his heart.

The barn suddenly seemed to close in on Charlie, the walls bearing down like ancient sentinels privy to secrets far darker than any human mind could comprehend. As Jessie crumpled to the ground, life ebbing away, the candle's pulsing light reached a crescendo, almost blinding in its intensity. The whisper that had clawed at the periphery of his thoughts coalesced into a single, seductive voice. It was mellifluous, beckoning, a siren call threading its way through the labyrinth of his mind.

Charlie looked down at the ancient book that Jessie had been so engrossed in. Its worn leather cover seemed to beckon to him, an old-world allure in contrast to the stark tragedy of the scene. The air in the barn felt thick, heavy with the weight of unrealized promises and shattered dreams. Each footstep towards the book felt like a betrayal of his principles, a dangerous dalliance with forces he couldn't comprehend.

His fingers brushed against the tome's cover, tracing the ornate, indecipherable glyphs etched onto its surface. And as he touched it, he felt a shiver run through his entire body, a cold electrical current that awakened senses he didn't know he had. It was as though the book were breathing life into the empty promises the voice had whispered, weaving tendrils of temptation around his rational mind.

The snow outside seemed to react to the events unfolding within the barn. It swirled in frenzied patterns, as if the heavens themselves were in upheaval, mirroring the tempest unfurling within him. With great effort, he closed the book, feeling the immediate retreat of the voice, its chilling sibilance fading away like mist before the dawn.

He stepped back, wrenching his hand away as if from a fiery flame, heart pounding in his chest. The book lay there, both innocent and malevolent, a Pandora's box of darkness and temptation. But the voice still echoed, not in the barn, but within the recesses of his mind, leaving him to ponder on the frayed edges of his own reality.

The surrounding air shuddered, as if the barn itself were breathing, and the world before Charlie's eyes dissolved into a haze. He found himself standing before a grave, the tombstone barely visible through the thick swirl of snow that enveloped the night. Without warning, the ground before the tombstone ruptured, and a decayed hand burst through the frozen soil, reaching for the world above.

His vision shifted, day replacing night, yet the scene played out again. Another grave, another hand. This time, sunlight filtering through leafy boughs illuminated the grotesque tableau. The horrifying clarity of these visions shook him to his core.

As reality snapped back into focus, Charlie found himself back in the barn, the air thick with the smell of decay and burned wax. His mind raced to connect the gruesome dots. These were the echoes of Jessie's dark rituals, but the voice, the entity, was playing a game with rules only it understood. Jessie was a pawn, his anguish manipulated to serve a cause far more malevolent. It didn't want to bring back Jessie's lost love; it wanted to raise the dead for its own insidious purpose.

The voice had been making promises it never intended to keep, at least not in a way that any human could desire. It whispered of life returned, but its real intention was an unholy resurrection, a betrayal of the natural order.

Charlie's eyes widened as a final vision engulfed him. Another graveyard materialized, this one shrouded in the gray light of dawn. The earth before a tombstone quivered, then erupted as another decayed form clawed its way out. The grotesque figure paused, as if taking its first unholy breath.

It was as if a curtain had been lifted from Charlie's eyes, the chilling clarity too potent to deny. Jessie's death had not been in vain, at least not for the entity that whispered promises. He had unwittingly become the last sacrifice, fulfilling his own dark ritual in a tragic, twisted irony.

Reality crashed back, and Charlie stood in the barn. The book still lay open on the floor, its ancient pages seeming to mock him. The voice, now silent, had completed its terrible work. Jessie's pain, his desperation, had been but a tool for something far more incomprehensible.

Charlie shook himself free of the crippling dread that gnawed at the edges of his consciousness. Action, he needed action. His eyes caught some dry kindling stacked against a wall. With shaky hands, he struck a match and set the wood ablaze. He turned and exited the barn, leaving behind Jessie, the ominous book, and the remnants of the malevolent ritual.

As the fire consumed the barn, its roaring flames seemed almost defiant against the cold air. The heat licked at his face, a stark contrast to the winter's bite. Sirens wailed in the distance, growing louder as they neared. Backup had finally arrived.

"Detective Langlois, what happened here?" one officer called out as they approached, their eyes widening at the inferno behind him.

Charlie looked back at the burning barn, then at his fellow officers. "We'll call it an accidental fire for now," he said, his voice tinged with a gravitas they had never heard before. "Get the fire department here to control it before it spreads."

As he stood there, bathed in the contrasting lights of the fire and the approaching dawn, Charlie couldn't shake the thoughts that swirled in his mind. There were evils beyond human understanding, horrors that lurked in the peripheries of our world. They whispered, they promised, and when given the chance, they broke through, leaving nothing but darkness in their wake. And while the fire could burn away the wood and the flesh, he knew it could not touch the shadows that now lived in his soul.

The Falls

The early morning light trickled through the frost-covered windows, illuminating the bedroom in a soft glow. George Connolly's eyes fluttered open, a gentle smile spreading across his face as he turned to Bea, lying beside him.

"Good morning, my love," George murmured, sitting up and stretching his arms.

Bea opened her eyes and returned his smile. "Morning, George. Looks like the storm has passed."

George pushed aside the quilt and stood up, his robe ready and waiting on the back of the door. Slipping into it, he turned back to Bea, "Are you excited for our walk today? It's a beautiful morning for it."

Bea nodded, her eyes twinkling. "Absolutely. I wouldn't miss our annual trek to the falls for the world, especially on my birthday."

He headed downstairs, each creak of the floorboards a testament to the years they'd spent in this home. Photographs adorned the walls: black and whites from their youth, colorful shots of birthdays, anniversaries, and countless trips to the falls.

Once in the kitchen, George set about making coffee as Bea took her usual spot at the kitchen table. The machine gurgled to life, filling the room with the rich aroma of brewing coffee.

"Ah, the elixir of life," George joked, glancing over at Bea.

"It wouldn't be a proper morning without it." She laughed.

George then turned his attention to making breakfast, Bea's favorite blueberry pancakes. "Nothing but the best for the birthday girl," he declared, flipping a pancake onto the hot griddle.

Bea watched, her eyes filled with warmth. "You spoil me, George."

"The snow is pretty deep this year, but I think we can make it to the falls," George noted, peering out the window at the winter wonderland the blizzard had created.

Bea responded with her usual unflagging enthusiasm, "A little snow never stopped us before."

With the pancakes done, George brought over two heaping plates and set them on the table. "Happy birthday, Bea," he said, taking his seat.

"Thank you, George," Bea replied, cutting into her pancake with delight.

As they ate, George felt a sense of comfort and happiness, looking forward to their walk to the frozen falls, a yearly tradition that, despite the many years behind them, never lost its magic.

After breakfast, George stood up and cleared the table. He glanced at Bea's plate, noting the untouched pancake.

"You didn't eat much, my love," he observed, a hint of concern coloring his voice.

"Oh, I guess I wasn't as hungry as I thought," Bea replied, her eyes meeting his. "Don't worry about it."

George nodded, taking the plates to the sink. The water roared to life, splashing over the ceramic dishes as he washed them one by one. Each plate, each fork, held memories of countless mornings like this one, of many treks to the falls, and days celebrated together.

"Well, no sense in letting good food go to waste," George commented, scraping the leftover pancake into a container and placing it in the fridge. "We'll need the energy for our walk, after all."

Bea laughed, "That's true, it's always quite the expedition."

With the kitchen now in order, George dried his hands and turned to Bea, "Shall we start getting ready, then?"

Her eyes gleamed with anticipation. "Absolutely, let's do it."

And so, as the winter sun climbed higher, bathing their cozy home in light, George felt a rush of happiness. Today was a special day, a continuation of a beloved tradition, and he couldn't wait to embark on their journey to the frozen falls.

George stepped into his boots, pulling them snugly against his ankles. As he zipped up his coat, his eyes caught sight of a small cedar box resting on the hall table. Picking it up gently, he felt its familiar weight in his hands and tucked it into the pocket of his heavy parka.

"Got everything?" Bea asked, pulling her scarf tight around her neck.

"I believe so," George said, holding open the door for her.

They stepped outside, and George was instantly grateful to see that their plow guy had already been by, clearing a path down the driveway. He breathed in deeply, inhaling the crisp, clean air. The world around them had been transformed overnight. Snow hung heavily on the branches of the towering pines, each needle intricately laced with ice. Silence that only comes after a heavy snowfall filled the air, a hushed stillness seemed to honor the beauty of the world.

"It's breathtaking, isn't it?" George said, his eyes scanning the winter wonderland before them.

"It always is," Bea replied, her eyes reflecting the pristine world around them. "Especially on days like today."

George nodded, feeling the significance of the moment of this annual ritual, settling deep within him. And so, with the cedar box securely in his pocket and Bea by his side, they began their slow and deliberate trek down toward the river, through a world made anew by winter's touch.

Gently navigating the recently plowed streets, George and Bea meandered their way through downtown Raven's Bend. The town seemed to be waking up, stretching its limbs after being blanketed by the storm. City Hall, with its towering clock tower, looked more dignified than ever with a dusting of snow accenting its stately lines.

"Remember the summer concert we attended there, must have been a decade ago?" George mused, pointing toward the city square in front of the building.

"Oh, I do," Bea said with a smile. "You danced like no one was watching."

Both chuckled at the memory, carrying it with them as they continued their walk. They soon passed *Through a Dark Mirror*, their favorite little cafe. The windows, decorated in a vintage speakeasy style, were foggy from the warmth inside, but they could make out the silhouettes of bundled-up patrons awaiting their food.

"Margaret must be in early today," Bea noted, recognizing the owner's customary winter shawl draped over a chair visible through the window. "You should stop by sometime."

"I definitely should," George agreed, his eyes catching the flicker of the 'Open' sign as they passed.

As they moved on, they approached the old, abandoned mill buildings that stood like ancient relics, casting long shadows over the frozen river below. Once vibrant hubs of industry, they now bore the patina of age and neglect. Yet in this light, covered in snow, there was a sense of reverence to them, as if they were holding onto countless untold stories.

"Even they look beautiful today," Bea observed, her eyes taking in the majestic dilapidation.

"Beauty in age and wisdom," George added, squeezing her hand.

Walking past the mill, they could see the river ahead, partially frozen and shimmering in the morning light, the promise of their destination pulling them forward. Raven's Bend was coming alive, but for George and Bea, this quiet journey through the heart of their town was a world unto itself. A world enriched by shared memories, annual traditions, and the simple but profound joy of being together.

As they reached the river walk, the pathways opened up to greet them, a striking panorama framed by skeletal trees and crisp, virgin snow. Folks were starting to make their way along the walkway, their breath misting the air as they passed.

"Morning, George," said Tom, a fellow longtime resident, as he jogged by in layers of thermal wear.

"Morning, Tom. Don't slip," George responded, nodding toward the icy patches still lurking in shaded areas.

"Will do," Tom called back, his jogging pace unfaltering despite the conditions.

An elderly couple passed by next, their hands securely wrapped around their walking sticks and a small poodle trailing behind them. George and Bea had seen them many times but had never learned their names.

"Beautiful day, isn't it?" George commented, eyeing the poodle's booties with amusement.

"Oh, it certainly is," replied the woman, her cheeks flushed from the cold.

Bea smiled warmly, a silent nod that needed no words to express the shared sentiment.

Each exchange, however brief, was an affirmation of community, a series of small anchors that rooted them to this place, to this time, to each other. The river walk was a communal space, but it was also deeply personal, a tapestry woven of countless steps, conversations, and memories. Today, as they made this sacred trek to the falls, George felt as if the town itself was part of their journey, cheering them on in a silent, wintry embrace.

As they rounded the last bend, the falls came into view, a spectacle of nature that took George's breath away every year. Encased in shimmering ice, the cascade appeared to be suspended in time, its once roaring torrents now a frozen tapestry. Layers of frost clung to the rock face, each icicle a delicate sculpture painstakingly crafted by the hands of winter.

The falls seemed to defy the very essence of their nature, ceasing their eternal tumble to stand still in crystalline splendor. The snow lent a softness to the scene, muting the jagged edges and adding a layer of serene purity. In this moment, it was as if the universe had pressed pause, capturing the falls in a prolonged instance of frigid beauty.

"It's as if time itself has stopped, don't you think, Bea?" George murmured, his eyes never leaving the stunning sight before them.

"Yes," Bea agreed softly, her voice barely more than a whisper carried away by the winter wind. "It's a moment captured forever, just like our memories, love."

George nodded, clutching the small cedar box a little tighter. Here, surrounded by the eternal freeze of the falls, he felt an ineffable sense of peace, a stillness that he knew could only be broken by the march of time. But for now, in this perfect moment, he was content.

As they neared the base of the falls, George's steps slowed, a hesitation creeping into his gait. His eyes were transfixed on the icy spectacle before them, as if wanting to hold on to this singular moment a little longer.

"Come on, George. Let's go up," Bea urged, her voice tinged with a gentle enthusiasm that he had come to know and love over the years.

Drawing a deep breath, George resumed his pace, each step a deliberate motion as they ascended the wooden staircase leading to the viewing deck above the falls. The steps were worn but sturdy, encrusted with a fresh layer of snow that crunched satisfyingly beneath their boots.

Reaching the top, they stepped onto the deck, its wooden boards covered in a thin blanket of snow, disturbed only by their footprints. From this vantage point, the frozen falls were even more majestic, the intricate patterns of ice and snow more apparent.

George placed the cedar box on the railing, his gloved hand resting atop it for a moment as he turned to Bea. "You always loved the view from up here."

"I still do, George," Bea replied, her eyes meeting his in a quiet, understanding gaze. "It's breathtaking."

"It is, indeed," George murmured, his heart swelling with a mix of love and nostalgia. And for a moment, under the frozen sky and overlooking the time-stopped falls, George felt a comforting warmth in the depth of winter's chill.

George's gaze dropped to the water below, where a dark pool had resisted the ice's complete embrace, leaving a window into the river's ceaseless flow. The water churned and gurgled, as if whispering secrets to the ice that sought to silence it.

"It's time, George," Bea's voice broke into his reverie, gentle yet resolute.

He looked at her, nodded, and then turned his attention to the cedar box that rested on the railing. His gloved hands lifted the lid, revealing the gray, powdery contents within. With a deep breath that misted in the frigid air, he took a handful of the ashes and held them over the open water.

"As you wished, my love," George whispered, and released the ashes. They floated down in a soft cascade, disappearing into the dark hole in the ice, becoming part of the river's eternal story.

"Goodbye, Bea. I love you," he whispered, his voice tinged with both sorrow and relief, as if unburdening a secret he'd held close for too long.

When he turned back, the space beside him on the deck was empty. Bea was gone, yet her presence remained in the falling snow, the icy sculptures, and the flowing water. And in the depths of his heart, where the memories of their life together would forever be his most treasured keepsakes.

As George descended the stairs and made his way back through the waking town of Raven's Bend, he knew that this annual pilgrimage was one he would make alone in the years to come. But for today, Bea had walked with him one last time, and that was enough. It was a solemn reminder that, despite the cruel passage of time and the harshness of loss, love remained, enduring, unyielding, and as constant as the river itself.

Loose Ends

"It was a solemn reminder that, despite the cruel passage of time and the harshness of loss, love remained, enduring, unyielding, and as constant as the river itself," Cora's voice trailed into the distance as it echoed throughout the cold air of the empty mill. She held her hands close to the fire as the light flickered across her pale skin. "Well, that's it. Well, most of it anyway."

"Did all of that really happen last night?" Mason asked. He looked out the broken window at the ice encrusted falls as the wind blowing in stung his face. "Was all of that true?"

"Truth?" Cora smiled. "All stories are true. Some may have happened. Some may yet to have happened." She waved her hand above the flames and continued, "And some may never happen. That's the beauty of a story. It holds a truth for whoever hears it."

"So, then back to my first question," Mason turned back to her, "did any of that happen last night?"

"Some of it did. Some of it was contained by telling the stories. By giving them an ear to hear, it kept them from holding place in the physical world."

"Some? What about all the deaths? David Allen? Is he dead buried beneath the ice within a few feet of his house? What about his warehouse? Did they really fend off a zombie attack?"

"Who knows?" Cora shrugged. "We will only find out once I finish the last story. Once I close that story, it will solidify the events of last night. Only then will we know the physical truth of the stories from the storm."

"I thought you said, 'That's it,' when you finished that last one about the falls. Is there more?" Mason held his hands to the flames, letting the warmth penetrate deep and cut the chill he still felt from the window.

"I did," Cora smiled. "There is still one story left to finish. Once it's done, once we determine if it will remain, I'll know what other debris from the storm will echo in this town."

"So, what's the last story?" Mason asked.

"Rarely, as I observe the stories and give them voice, do I find myself interacting with them. The funny thing about stories is that most of the time, they don't realize they are part of a narrative. They don't know they are telling a tale with their mere existence. Some will try to run from their destiny. Some embrace it. And some will try to deny it." She stood and faced the window, looking away from Mason.

"What's the final story?" Mason asked as he stood and joined Cora at the window.

"Tell me, Mason," she said as glints of sunlight danced across her face from spiderweb cracks in the window, "what do you remember about your life?"

"What do you mean?"

"Where did you grow up? When did you find yourself in Raven's Bend? What do you remember from your youth?"

"I don't understand why you're asking," Mason shook his head and rubbed his temples as he felt a slight headache spawning in the recesses of his brain.

"Mason, think on your past," Cora faced him and placed a comforting hand on his shoulder.

"I was born in Maine. Right in Durham. After I served in the Marines, I was down on my luck and found myself up here taking care of my mom, but after she passed, I never got my shit back together and I've been living off the streets for the past eight years." Mason squirmed beneath the icy gaze of Cora.

"Have you now?" She asked, her voice boring deep within his brain.

"This isn't funny," Mason's voice cracked. "I'm real. I know I'm alive."

"My dear Mason," Cora raised her hand to touch Mason's face, "a story is no more or less real than anything else. Everything about you tells a story. I'm here to figure out if your story will remain written into the fabric of the real world or if you will be reabsorbed into the realm of dreams."

"I know who I am! I have memories," Mason shouted as he pulled away from Cora's touch.

"All memories are stories, in their own right, and all stories are memories, aren't they? When we tell stories, we are remembering something and weaving that into the fabric of the waking world. We speak the stories into being and they take on a life of their own as they interact with those who hear the stories." She paused and looked out over the falls, icy flows glinting with a bright white glow, "You are struggling right now. Trying to determine if you are a dreamer or a dream. Am I right?" She twirled her hand over the dust on the windowsill as it lifted and swirled in a familiar pattern, sparkling and glinting in the shafts of sunlight breaking into the mill.

Behind his eyes, Mason felt the tug again. The same tug he felt before at Cora's words. He felt the draw of the story.

"Yes. Please tell me. Am I real or am I a story?" Mason asked, shaking his head.

"What if I told you it doesn't matter? What if I told you everyone was one or the other at various points?"

"I need to know. Please tell me," Mason's hands gripped the windowsill, his knuckles white with the effort.

"Mason, you are real. Being a story doesn't change that. When we finish here, you may remain in the world or you may return to the Sove, but, Mason, you must accept your fate, whatever it may be. I don't know if you'll remain or if you'll return, but I can tell you that you must move on. We have to finish this page of your story." Cora walked to the door and held out her hand. "Follow me. Let's take our leave of this old place. My ancient bones are old, and I find myself growing tired."

Mason took her hand and listlessly followed her to an unbarred door leading outside.

"What's next?" He asked, looking at the crack of light bleeding in around the door frame.

"I honestly do not know. I can only see your story up to this point. To this door. This is the last page of this chapter. What's next for you? I do not know. I just know that one of two things will happen when you step through this doorway. You return to the Sove and await a new story…"

"Or?" Mason asked, his voice rising in intensity.

"Or you continue your story here."

"But what if I'm not real?"

"Mason," Cora lightly taps his hand, "you must remove that phrase from your vocabulary. You are real. Your story is real. If you return to the Sove, then you return. If you remain here, you will have always been."

"I don't understand. I'm sorry."

"When a rogue story is folded into this realm, it is as if it has always existed. Every bit of your history has always been. Every interaction you had has existed. Think of it as rewrites to the story of the waking world. Nothing will change. I'm not even sure you will remember this conversation today."

"But what if it's the end of my story?" Mason pulled his hand from Cora's.

"It's never the end. It's just change. All stories change. If you're not telling your story by living life here, then you'll do it as part of the Sove. Nothing really ends. Not as long as stories remain."

"You promise?" Mason took a step closer to the door.

"Mason, I promise. Whatever your next step is, I will be beside you. We will either walk out into Raven's Bend together, or we will step into the Sove. Are you ready?" Her voice fell soft into the room as she whispered.

"I'm ready. I think." He stepped closer to the door as Cora opened it. The faint line of light bleeding in around the rough edges of the wood grew, bathing the room in a bright white light. The sunlight washed out everything beyond the door in a uniform white, like a curtain of light hung on the doorframe.

"Then let's go. Let's find your story," Cora said as she pulled his hand and led Mason through the opening.

As their silhouettes shrank and vanished in the bright sunlight, the door swung inward of its own accord. As it pivoted slowly on its hinges, the light narrowed and narrowed until only a sliver remained outlining the door and the wind whistled through the cracks of the old mill, blowing dust and echoing through the abandoned corridors.

Afterword

Thanks so much for taking the time to read these stories. I hope you've enjoyed. If you did be sure to let me know on social media or drop me a review on Amazon.

I'd like to wrap things up by giving some background on some of these stories.

The collection began when I was putting together stories for my first collection, The Albatross. Down from the Mountain and One Mile Home both took place during a blizzard, and both took place in my fictional town of Raven's Bend, Maine. It started to sink into my headcanon that they took place on the same night during the same storm.

And thus, One Snowy Night was born.

I envisioned a set of stories taking place in The Bend. Some of them connected to each other. Others independent stories. And some even connected to earlier works of mine. If you are one of my readers who picks up on those connections, kudos to you.

And for those not in the know, Raven's Bend is my fictional stand-in for the Lewiston/Auburn area of Maine. So, for those of you familiar with this area, you may have noticed some landmarks and people that seem familiar.

The Woman and the Mill and Loose Ends

I'm a sucker for framing stories. If you've read The Albatross, you know that already. Just as The Albatross is framed by a beginning and end to justify you sitting down to read the stories, so does the first and last entry in this collection frame and give a reason for the other stories. I loved stories like Bradbury's "Illustrated Man" where there was a justification for the immersion of the reader into the stories as if they were being dragged along with someone within the story.

In the Loop

This story is a play on the whole time loop motif. I wanted to give a spin on it without an explanation. I just wanted to explore Daisy's feelings as she drove headfirst into the storm.

Around the Bend

This was a fun one to write. Occasionally, I like to try and stretch myself and see if I can go outside my wheelhouse of horror, sci-fi, and fantasy and write a real-world story. I think this one fits the bill.

Down from the Mountain

This was written as part of a writing prompt for a writing community I was a part of and was originally featured in a seasonal winter-themed anthology published by Wolfsinger Publishing, and later republished in my collection The Albatross and Other Tales. The prompt for this one was to write a story incorporating gods into the modern age.

The Four Connected Stories

The next four stories started as just the one: One Mile Home. This story, originally featured in The Albatross, is based on a true story about me (except I didn't die), but also serves as a springboard into the next few stories in this collection. The climax of the storm, so to speak. OMH introduces the warehouse, while the Plow sets the stage for what happens during Third Shift Woes (which I can neither confirm nor deny the existence of zombies at a warehouse distribution center in the Lewiston/Auburn area), and The Overpass serves as a closing to the whole ordeal.

The Falls

This brings us to the last story before the closing. This one is very personal. This story is about saying goodbye and serves as a mirror story to In the Loop. This collection, and this story in particular, is dedicated to my father-in-law. I wrote this story, a story of saying goodbye to someone after they are gone with him in mind the entire time. A lot of who I am as a writer and some of the direction that this book took was based on his input. Outside of my partner, my father-in-law was the first person who knew about the idea for One Snowy Night. I wish he had gotten the chance to read it. I know he would have loved it.

Thanks again for reading my stories. If you enjoyed them, be sure to stop by on Facebook or Instagram to let me know.

You can find me online at:

- adfarr.com

- Facebook.com/AnthonyDFarr

- <u>Instagram.com/adfarrwrites</u>

MORE CHILLS FROM VELOX BOOKS

MORE CHILLS FROM VELOX BOOKS

www.ingramcontent.com/pod-product-compliance
Lightning Source LLC
Chambersburg PA
CBHW030147010826
48973CB00002B/762